FIRE & FLOOD

FIRE & FLOOD

MOUNT OLYMPUS ACADEMY BOOK 1

KATE KARYUS QUINN   DEMITRIA LUNETTA
MARLEY LYNN

LITTLE FISH PUBLISHING

For anyone still waiting for their Hogwart's letter to arrive - this book is for you.

1

My parents and sister are at the airport, getting ready to board a plane headed toward Greece. Meanwhile, I'm waiting to be checked out of the hospital.

I'm supposed to be on that flight with them—a three-month work trip that my archeologist mom organized. But two weeks earlier I came down with a virus that turned into pneumonia. This, combined with my lifelong mortal enemy, asthma, made breathing suddenly a lot harder. And then nearly impossible.

That's where the hospital comes in.

The doctors saved my life. And then totally ruined it by telling my parents I should stay home tucked under a blanket on my grandmother's couch so I could be all rested up for my senior year of high school come fall.

I honestly didn't think they would really go without me. No offense to my grandma, but she's pretty old and kinda wobbly. No way would my parents leave their sickly daughter with her while they were on a totally different continent.

"Leave me behind? Screw that," I'd laughed right after the doctor who gave me the bad news left the room.

No one else laughed. Mom, Dad, and my older sister Mavis just stared back at me.

I swallowed, not liking those looks. "Right?"

"Well, sweetheart—" Mom paused as she took off her glasses and began to clean them on the hem of her shirt. It's one of her favorite avoidance tactics. When I was ten and asked her what sex was, she polished so long and hard that she snapped them in half.

Suddenly I was worried.

"Dad?" I turned to my no-bullshit go-to guy.

"Sweetheart, we rented out our house. Not to mention that for Mom, it's a work trip."

"And I'm getting college credits for an internship," Mavis added. That one really stung. Mavis and I have always been close. Sure there's the usual sisterly bickering, but beneath that we genuinely like each other. I was looking forward to spending the summer together exploring Greece with her and hearing about her first year of college out in California. All year she only came home for Christmas and I missed her like crazy. But now she's heading off again. Without me.

I argued—eloquently, I believe, or as eloquently as someone who has to suck on an inhaler when they get too worked up—for my right to go on this trip. Sure, it was about having fun, but it was also about education, and opportunity and... and the fact that I'd already rubbed it in all my ex-friends' faces that I was going.

In the end, we compromised. And by compromised I mean they just decided.

They would go to Greece as planned.

I would stay with Grandma and she would teach me how to knit. Which was also, Mom pointed out, a learning opportunity. They presented me with a big cotton bag filled with a rainbow's worth of yarn and my very own pair of knitting needles.

It was one hell of a consolation prize. But I wasn't raised to be a sore loser, so I forced a smile and a thank you. Somehow I even managed to wish them well on their travels. Did an evil voice deep inside wish them months of chronic diarrhea? Maybe. But at least I didn't say it aloud.

Maybe I can knit them some diapers.

Now, I hold my bag of knitting supplies as a nurse wheels me out to the curb where my grandma waits behind the wheel of her '85 Lincoln. As I settle myself in the passenger seat my phone bings with a text.

MAVIS: We just boarded.

MAVIS: Didn't get seats together, but luckily I've already made friends.

A pic follows this second text. Mavis and some unbelievably good-looking guy grinning into the camera.

That is so typical Mavis. Even her bad luck turns out good. Stuck by herself and ends up next to one of the hottest guys in the universe.

The car jerks sideways and thumps up onto the curb and then down again. My phone flies out of my hand.

"Almost got that sonofabitch!" Grandma yells, giving her steering wheel a slap that I can't decide is meant to be congratulatory or an admonishment. I look back to see an alligator sunning himself beside the ditch at the side of the road. Gran hates them ever since they ate her Bichon Frise, Elsa, and attempts to mow them down with her car whenever possible. "Next time, next time," she mutters.

"Hey Grandma," I say, in my best poor pathetic left behind tone of voice. "Maybe I can drive the rest of the way home? Get some practice in? It would really lift my spirits."

Grandma shoots me a look that is clearly meant to convey she may be seventy-three, but she ain't senile yet. "Sweetheart, you've failed that driving test what is it...eight times now? Didn't the last tester beg you to quit before you killed someone?"

"Grandma, I know how to drive," I protest. "I'm just a bad test taker."

I'm actually epically terrible. I tend to freeze up in high stress situations. And there is no situation more stressful than trying to go where you want without having to beg Mom or Dad for a lift.

"You're sick, Edie. What kind of grandma do you think I am? Why not rest a little bit on the way home? You look a little peaked." The light changes and Grandma floors it, slamming me back into my seat.

Another battle lost. It's true, though, I am tired. I close my eyes and try to pretend I'm on a plane. It's lifting up into the sky, to travel across an ocean, before finally settling down in the land where gods were born.

As we pull into the parking lot behind Grandma's condo the typical Florida afternoon downpour begins. Grandma slowly totters along while holding her little old lady umbrella that she always keeps in her handbag over my head so I don't get soaked and end up back in the hospital. It's nice and all, but I'm about three feet taller than Grandma so I end up just kind of walking hunched over to get under the umbrella, which doesn't make my chest feel too hot.

Finally we get into the creaky old elevator. It grumbles and lurches its way up to the sixth floor. By the time Grandma unlocks the door all I want to do is cry.

"What's that face for?" Dad asks.

I gasp. He's seated at Grandma's breakfast bar with a cup of coffee. Not on a plane to Greece—but here.

"You stayed!" I rush forward, throwing my arms around him. "I knew you wouldn't leave without me. Where are Mom and Mavis? Are they mad they missed their trip?"

The look on Dad's face as he peels away from me tells me everything I need to know. "Edie, it was Mom's grant. And her dream. You know that. Asking her to miss this chance..."

I swallow hard. Force a nod. "Right. I know."

And I do know. Mom met Dad when they were both studying abroad in Greece years ago. They fell in love, she got pregnant, and Mom decided to stay home with us kids and give up her career until we were older. I never really understood it. Why couldn't she do both?

When I ask Mom she'll only says she was overly worried about our safety just like any young mom. Really, though, Dad's always been the more overprotective one, while Mom is constantly pushing me to let go and embrace my wild side. I've tried to tell her I don't have a wild side, that I'm pretty sure I was born without one. That's when she gets this glint in her eye and insists that someday I'm going to surprise myself. If Mavis is around she always like to add, "In bed." Ha ha ha, Mavis.

Anyway, once I started high school, Mom decided it was time to pick up where she left off. She finished her degree and then this opportunity to work in Greece came up. Dad didn't like it. They tried to hide the fact they were arguing, but even though neither of them are screamers, there's always a certain tone to their voices when they're upset. Eventually Mom won and well, it was immediately obvious how excited she was. Suddenly Greece this and Greece that was all Mom could talk about.

So yeah, unless I was on my deathbed, there's no way Mom wasn't getting on that airplane. And Mavis, well, she was always Mom's favorite, while I've always been Dad's.

I hug Dad again. "Thank you for coming back for me."

He ruffles my hair. Or tries. It's wet, so he just sort of rubs my head instead. "Well, I had to decide who needed more help staying out of trouble—you or your mom. You won, but only just barely."

"Hey, Dad," I smile up at him. "Speaking of trouble... since we're here all summer with nothing to do, maybe you can help me get more driving practice in."

"Aw, baby girl." Dad smiles fondly. "I would rather spend an afternoon wrestling alligators then be inside a vehicle you're driving."

"Dad!"

"But I did have an idea." He rummages in his pocket and then holds up two laminated cards with a ta-da expression.

"Those are bus passes."

"Yup. Good all summer. I figured, well, maybe we could explore the public transportation system in our fair city. It's eco-friendly and it'll be an adventure!"

I stare at Dad. He is working so hard to sell this. Only the vice principal of a junior high school would be this excited about bus passes, and only a monster would burst his bubble.

"Wow. Bus passes and knitting. Best summer ever." Somehow I manage to keep most of the sarcasm out of my voice.

Dad grins back at me. "Best summer ever," he echoes.

Thing is, I think he means it.

2

That night I have a terrible nightmare. I can't breathe, like when I have an asthma attack but a hundred times worse. I realize I'm underwater. My grandmother floats by, her eyes vacant. She's dead. I wake clawing at my throat. Dad finds me sobbing on the floor.

Inhaler in hand, he makes me take three deep breaths to calm my breathing.

"It's okay, it's just the medicine you're taking. It gives you bad dreams."

"It was so real." I tell him. "I thought I was drowning. Grandma—"

"Your grandma is fine. She's sleeping."

He gets me back to bed and stays with me until I fall asleep again. It takes a while. The cold feel of the ocean is in my bones.

After a couple of days of rest I'm back to normal. It's actually fun living on the beach with Grandma. She has a bunch of kooky friends. They beach walk every morning and knit in the afternoon. Although I think their knitting circle is just an excuse to day drink and gossip.

My dad and I start taking bus trips together. We go to historical sites and then find the best beach bungalows to eat seafood. It rains a lot, even for Florida, and Dad is terrified I'm going to catch a cold or worse again. He gets me a full body rain coat that is stifling in the humid Florida heat.

Every so often he oh so casually asks if I want to give Bronwyn or Toby a call and see if they want to come along. The first few times I mumble something about them being busy, but finally I can't take it anymore.

"Dad, we're not friends anymore. Okay? I have no friends. I am a social pariah. So let's just go to the home of the world's largest milkshake and make ourselves sick drinking them. Sound good to you?"

Of course, Dad being Dad, he couldn't let it go. He waited until we were trapped on the bus together to ask, "Wanna tell me what happened?"

No, I really didn't. How could I explain that I got drunk and kissed the star of the lacrosse team? A guy I'd been crushing on for two years. A guy who was currently dating someone else. But that's not even the worst part. Our kiss gave him some sort of weird rash. All around his mouth and lips—even his tongue—it looked like he'd been burned or something. He told the whole school I'd given him gonorrhea. And then two other guys on the lacrosse team said I'd given it to them too.

Just like that, I wasn't just a slut. I was a dirty skank. Never mind that I've never had sex with anyone. And that this was only, like, my third kiss. Not that anyone would believe that. My friends didn't drop me so much as slowly back away, until they were just specks in the distance.

No one came to visit me during my week in the hospi-

tal. That's when I realized this wasn't going to blow over. I'd
sorta nurtured a dream that Mom would love Greece so
much she'd insist we stay and I'd finish out my last year of
high school there. But that's obviously not going to
happen.

"Hey, Edie." Dad nudges me. "Whatever it is, you can tell
me. I'm a cool dad, remember?"

I laugh. My dad is such a huge dork.

I tell him an edited version of the story—minus the
drinking and gonorrhea. And he says all the right things.
How it takes two to kiss and how that boy was the one
cheating on his girlfriend. Finally he kisses my forehead.

"You're young. You're allowed to make mistakes."

And then we drink milkshakes so big we have to
unbutton our pants for the bus ride back to Grandma's.

Once a week we Skype with Mom and Mavis and it's
always the worst part of the week. Mavis is tan and
glowing and has five different gorgeous Greek boys madly in
love with her. She tells me about each one in great detail.
Including the hot guy who was on the flight with her—
Nico. If he's anything to go by, Greece has the hottest boys
on the planet.

Halfway through the summer, I start to dread Skype day.
Mom never seems totally into it. It's weird, almost like she's
nervous to stay on the line too long. I can tell it irritates Dad,
but he won't say anything to her about it, or at least not
when I'm in the room. There are definitely some lowered
tones when I walk away, but I try not to eavesdrop. If they're
fighting, that's their thing.

I'm actually relieved one day when Dad says no one's
picking up. Dad freaks, though, and tries to connect five

more times. Each time there is no answer he becomes more upset.

"They're just busy," I say. "Mavis probably has a new boyfriend and Mom—"

"No." Dad cuts in, his voice sharp. "Your mother wouldn't. We had a deal. She couldn't miss a Skype. I didn't want to worry that she'd gone missing."

"Missing? Why would she go missing?" I stare at Dad. "What are you talking about?"

He blinks, as if seeing me and remembering I'm his daughter. "I meant if she got lost while sightseeing. I'm just…I'm going to call her cell. I'm sure it's a time thing." His phone is already in his hand as he speaks. There's no way I'm getting any more answers out of him.

Later tonight we're going to an all-you-can-eat place called the Shrimp Shack. I'll ask him again on the bus about the Mom going missing thing. Being stuck in a confined space and questioned ruthlessly can work both ways.

Dad scrubs his face and mutters, "Not answering. Damn it."

"Dad?" I ask. He doesn't seem to hear me, too engrossed in whatever he's typing into his phone.

Deciding to give him some space, I step out onto the balcony.

Grandma is already on the boardwalk with her friends. Even from the sixth floor she's easy to spot with her bright orange sun hat.

"Hey!" I call out, waving to get their attention. One of her friends catches sight of me and nudges Grandma. Soon there's five old people waving wildly.

I am still laughing when I see it.

My hands freeze in midair. Dogs in the condos all

around us begin to bark madly. It's like they can sense what's coming.

A wall of water in the ocean.

"Grandma!" I scream. "Run!"

Sirens begin to wail. Grandma and her friends finally see what's rolling in behind them and just stare in shock. Finally, they get moving, scrambling back toward the building. I lean over the balcony, watching as they disappear beneath the awning below.

From behind, strong arms wrap around me. My father pulls me away from the railing and yells, "We have to get higher up." He jerks me back into the condo and then shuts the sliding glass door, flipping the flimsy lock—as if that will keep out what's coming.

I can't tear my eyes away from it. It's a wave unlike anything I've ever seen before. I could swear I see the shape of a person. A giant foamy head with leering mouth and two long arms reaching forward. I blink and shiver as two great watery hands slam against the beach.

The condo shudders.

We run to the condo doorway and I turn back in time to witness the wave's face slam against the glass door. It shatters—shards of glass and water mixing as they tumble through the air—and time slows.

The glass flies toward me. I freeze, unable to move, once again proving Mavis's theory that I'd be the first to die in a zombie movie. Closing my eyes, I scream; the sound burns and scrapes at my throat.

"Edie, c'mon," Dad tugs at my hand.

I cough and a puff of smoke comes out of my mouth. The glass and water that had been flying at me are gone, leaving only wafts of steam.

I barely have time to process this as Dad grabs my shoulders and pulls me through the doorway. Water pools around our feet as we rush for the stairs. The sea rains down on us, the stairway becoming a river. The current is strong but Dad goes first to take the brunt of the force and I struggle behind him, using the railing to pull myself up.

When we reach the eighth floor, the water breaks—the wave must not have been this tall—and we tiredly make our way up to the top of the building and out onto the roof. The rooftop greenhouse gleams in the sunlight, but no one is inside. We're the only ones up here. Are we the only ones who made it?

I collapse, drained, and Dad hugs me. "It's okay," he says as I shiver against him. "You're in shock. You're okay," he repeats. He thought to grab my inhaler, or had it on him, and places it in my mouth.

"Deep breath," he tells me.

I nod and inhale, letting the medicine open my lungs. I also let myself cry a little.

I come back to myself slowly. Where did that wave come from? Why was there no warning? What happened to my grandma and all her friends?

"Grandma!" I yell, struggling to my feet. I rush to the edge of the building.

"No, don't look," Dad yells after me, but I have to see.

I look out over Cape Athena and freeze. There's water as far as the eye can see, with buildings poking out and cars bobbing to the surface.

The ocean has swallowed the land.

3

Again, I think of my grandmother.

"Maybe she was able to grab hold of something," I say, even though I know it's unlikely. Dad knows who I mean.

"Yeah," he agrees, his hands landing on my shoulders. "She's a wily old lady. I wouldn't count her out."

I lean back into Dad as more tears leak out and the water swirls below us.

"Edie, sweetheart, I know this isn't a great time, but in case anything should happen to me—"

I whirl around to stare. "Nothing's going to happen to you."

Dad nods. "I hope not. But this—he spreads an arm wide, indicating the devastation around us— "Florida doesn't get tsunamis or tidal waves, or whatever that was."

"It's global warming. Crazy weather and storms and..." I'm desperate for an explanation.

"I don't think so, not this time." Dad sounds so certain. "This...this is something else."

The image of that face in the water flashes across my

mind. I push it away. "I don't understand. What else could it be?"

Dad hesitates for a long moment. "Mom and I always told you that you were named after my Great Aunt Edith. But that isn't true. I don't even have a Great Aunt Edith. I don't have any family at all, except for Mom, Mavis, and you."

I am suddenly more scared than when we were running from the water. This moment feels too big. I swallow and try to make a joke. "Are we clearing our consciences before we die? If so, I should probably tell you—remember several years ago when the old globe in your study broke? Well, it was me, not Mavis, who broke it. I wanted to see how fast I could spin it and well, it went pretty fast before it fell off your desk."

Dad doesn't laugh.

I nudge him, desperately needing his grim expression to change. "C'mon, you're not withholding forgiveness in our final moments. Are you?"

Dad takes my hands. "Edie, I know you're not ready for this. But we've run out of time and you need to know who you are."

"I know who I am." I hold up my inhaler. "Asthma. Chronic bad back. Oddly good at knitting. I'm basically seventeen going on seventy."

Dad shakes his head. "No. Edie. You need to listen. Your mother named you. Your re—"

The whole world shakes and rumbles. I stumble and Dad catches me.

"Not another wave," I cry, searching the empty horizon.

"Edie." Dad's hands clench around my arms. "Run for the stairs. Go down to our floor but stay in the hallway.

Away from all windows." He releases me with a push. "Go now! Hurry!"

Running is not an asthmatic's strong suit. Especially after how quickly we got up the stairs. I kind of jog-walk down the stairs, then take a break on the third landing. There's running and shouting in the hallway, and I hear a dog barking excitedly, reminding me of Grandma's dead Bichon Frise and Grandma's silver head disappearing under the awning and...

"Shit," I say, slamming my shoulder into the door for our floor. A rogue wave doesn't just happen. There had to have been an earthquake somewhere. Are there earthquakes in Greece? Mom wasn't answering her phone.

I grab my phone from the counter—remarkably it isn't wet—and go right to Twitter. #RogueWave is trending and #CapeAthena. Everyone is marking themselves safe and there are endless thoughts and prayers flying around. What I don't see is reports of an earthquake anywhere, or a missed call on my phone. In the age of instant news, Mom and Mavis didn't check in when they knew our condo took a direct hit from a tsunami.

That's not a good sign.

My phone goes off and for a split second my heart leaps, certain it's Mom.

But it's Dad, FaceTiming me.

I hold up my screen, ready to share my fears, no matter how bad, when I see it's not just Dad in the picture. He's in the greenhouse up on the roof, plants thick and heavy on all sides of him. There's another face behind his, wet, dripping —pure water itself. It's on the other side of the greenhouse glass. I can see it pressed up against the window, pulsing. It's like the face I saw in the wave, but detached just standing behind my...

"Dad?" I ask, my voice quiet and unsure.

"Edie, listen to me," Dad says. "If somebody comes to you and tells you to go with them, do NOT do it."

"Um, duh?" I say, wondering if this is more side effects of my medication. Surely there isn't some water specter standing behind my dad while he talks to me about stranger danger.

"Unless they say the word *ichor*. Do you understand?"

"Icky?" Yes, I am definitely hallucinating. Dad is telling me to only go with icky people. I let out a wild, high pitched giggle.

"Ichor," Dad repeats patiently. "I. C. H. O. R." Behind him, a crack starts to appear in the glass.

"Edie, I'm sorry. I wish I had time to explain—"

But he doesn't. The glass breaks, the face pushing through and overtaking Dad in a wall of water. His phone shorts out and I'm standing in our living room staring at a black screen, just saying the word *dad*, over and over and over.

4

Okay. Okay. Okay.

Mom and Mavis are incommunicado.

Dad is—I'm not ready to think about that yet.

Which leaves Grandma. Dad told me to stay away from windows, and there's no way the water has gone down yet, but it must have. I can hear other people now, voices rising up from the beach. If people are outside, surely I can be near a window?

I look out. Tentatively. The water *has* receded. The beach is littered with all kinds of things that rolled from further inland when the water swept back out to sea. There's a car on its side, basically everyone's patio furniture, a lot of bicycles, and a bunch of huge umbrellas from all the outdoor restaurants. I spot a bright orange hat and let out a gasp. Grandma.

But first, I've got to at least try the roof. My legs tremble as I trudge up the stairs for the second time. It's not just the exercise. I'm scared. If I was watching myself in a movie I'd be screaming, "Don't go on the roof, you dummy!"

I hesitate at the door and then, giving the handle a twist, come bursting out.

"Auuughh!" I scream in full warrior mode. Or try to, but my lungs can't muster more than a squeak.

It's all for nothing. And no one.

The greenhouse is entirely gone, broken glass and torn plants scattered across the rooftop. There's the wreck of the metal frame, twisted and gruesome, but that's it. No Dad. No trace. Almost like the water just came and swept him off the roof, but that's not possible.

I walk to the edge of the roof and look at the building across the street. The bricks are only wet about twenty feet up. The water didn't get as high as the roof, no way.

I close my eyes and remember Dad's expression on that FaceTime call. Intent. Focused. Scared. He knew that water face *thing* was out there. Hunting him.

But that can't be possible. Dad is the stuffy vice-principal. An evil water monster is not gonna come after a guy who makes dad jokes and dreams of someday retiring to play the competitive Scrabble circuit. I mean, right?!?

I shift every torn leaf and chunk of metal I can, looking for some clue that he's still alive. Looking for some hope.

I finally find it beneath a piece of glass that I carefully use the toe of my shoe to flip aside. Dad's cell phone. The screen is cracked, but when I pick it up a picture of my own face smiles up at me. Dad is beside me in the pic, half cut off because he's terrible at taking selfies. It's from our last bus ride. Tears well up, blinding me. I scrub them away and type in Dad's code. The phone doesn't unlock. I try until it locks me out.

"Shit. Shit. Shit."

I used his phone last night to order dinner. He never

changes his code. It's the month Mavis was born and the month I was born. 0309. When and why did he change it?

The sun is beating down and I know there's nothing more up here. I take the stairs all the way down, hoping Dad will be at the bottom, wondering where I am. With Grandma at his side. I hold onto this hope as I navigate the stairs. They're a wreck; fish and sand and seaweed make them slippery and I have to be careful not to fall.

It takes forever but I make my way down to the lobby. A few people are gathered there already, talking and crying and praying.

Passing them, I make my way out to the beach, broken glass and bits of torn up pavement shredding my sandals in seconds. By the time I'm past the worst I'm barefoot, the wet sand strangely cool on my aching feet.

I just walk for a little bit, searching faces. Everyone is looking for someone, people are calling names, people looking for their dogs, and dogs looking for their owners. I spot a cat sitting high in a windowsill, tail twitching in the sun, completely unconcerned.

"Dick," I say, and I swear it looks right at me.

I see dads and moms and children all finding each other, a lot of joyful reunions. But not me. I haven't found Grandma. What I do find is a line of yarn, drawn tight in the sand. It's a bright orange, the same color Grandma had been using to make an afghan for the minister's wife. The one I *don't* like, she kept saying.

I follow the yarn, and it leads me right back to the condo, under the awning where I saw Grandma run for safety. I thought she'd made it, and Dad had said not to count her out, but I've been looking for Grandma for at least an hour, and something tells me I should have found her by now.

When I enter the building I see the yarn leading up to the elevator. The doors are closed, the yarn pinched tight. There are a bunch of men working around it, talking excitedly. They get quiet when they see me, and my chest gets even tighter.

"What happened?" I ask.

The men look at each other, one of them finally decides to take the plunge. "The elevator...it looks like she was trying to go up, to the sixth floor."

"That's where she lives," I tell them. "My grandma."

One of the guys take his hat off. My heart sinks.

"She didn't make it," I say, almost to myself.

"No," another guy says. "She did, but..."

My heart leaps, hoping Grandma is fine. Except he said but.

"But what?" I ask, desperate.

He pauses, not wanting to tell me more. That's when I spot the blood, just starting to seep from inside the closed doors, tinging the orange yarn a dark red.

"It fell." I finish for him. "It fell six floors." I sink to the ground and am comforted by strangers.

It's been a few hours and everyone is being really nice to me. Mostly because it looks like I'm the only person that lost someone. Lost everything. I try to tell people about the second wave, the one that took Dad. I say "wave" instead of "water face" because people are already worried enough about my mental and emotional state. But nobody saw a second wave, and eventually I figure out the EMS people are not going to let me go back up to the room if I don't start making sense.

So I try. I tell them no, I'm just confused. Dad was definitely swept away by that first wave, and Grandma died in the elevator. Her friends find me, tell me they had warned her away from the elevator, but that she couldn't get up the steps fast enough with her hip, and she had to get to me, immediately.

She didn't. They know that. I know that.

They all say what they think will help—EMS people, condo management, Grandma's friends. That it will be okay. That it was an act of God. That it's a good thing my mother and sister are away and are safe.

There's some talk about me being a minor and not able to stay alone, but there's a ton of confusion—lots of damage and minor injuries to take care of—so I just slip away and go back upstairs.

I shut the door, happy to put something solid between me and the rest of the world. I collapse on the couch, grabbing my phone again and hoping to see that Mavis called. Or Mom. Something. Neither has posted on social media in the last twenty four hours.

There's no one. Nothing.

I sit on the couch as the sky grows dark. I play back the day, rewriting different parts. I tell Grandma not to go for her walk. We don't go all the way up to the roof. When Dad tells me to run, I insist on staying with him. Instead of Face-Timing me, Dad gets away from the water monster. Why did Dad waste his time with that anyway? Or why didn't he say the normal things? Stuff like I love you. Instead, I got *ichor*. Whatever that means.

Ichor. The word echoes in my head. I can hear Dad spelling it out.

My body stiff, I shift to pull my phone from my pocket. I do another Mom and Mavis check, which again comes up empty, before Googling *ichor*.

"What?" I stare at my screen.

It means *blood of the gods*.

I tense. One of the back spasms that's plagued me my whole life, pulses through me. I cry out in pain. Dad always make me lie on the floor when this happens, so that's what I do now.

I lie on my back, stare at the ceiling, and wait for this to pass.

5

Six Months Later

Mom and Mavis are still missing. I've been told the Greek police force is stumped. They seem to have disappeared without a trace.

People say to have someone you love go missing and not have answers is the worst. But they're wrong. The worst is when you get the call that your father's body has washed up on the beach ten miles north of where he was last seen. The worst is going to the morgue to identify him. The worst is having to make the decision to bury him next to Grandma.

The worst is my life.

I have foster people now. I refuse to refer to them as family.

They're not so bad. But they're not so great either. Thank God I'm seventeen and only have to do this for a year.

I think they had this idea about really making a difference in someone's life. Carla, that's the lady, told me on the first day, "We're gonna get your inner light shining again."

But that light is permanently burned out, so far as I can

tell. And I like it that way. I don't want to feel. I don't want to think. And I sure as shit don't want to shine.

I can tell Carla and her husband, Rod, are disappointed with me. I'm a dark little rain cloud drifting through their beautiful house full of beautiful things. They're art collectors and dealers. Expensive and strange sculptures seem to be their specialty. Expensive and strange and *delicate*. If I get within breathing distance of anything they immediately cry out, "Ah, don't touch that! It's delicate!"

This weekend, though, I have the house to myself. Carla and Rod are on an all-day buying trip. I could tell they were nervous about leaving me alone with all their precious art for so long. The last thing Rod said was, "Uh, just so you know, most people wouldn't understand the true value of what we have here. If you took one of these sculptures, like say 'Wisdom' right here"—he gestured to a sculpture that looked like a pile of human teeth. "If you took that to the local pawn shop they wouldn't give you anything for it."

"Don't worry, I wasn't planning on pawning anything while you were gone," I told him.

Rod let out this big fake laugh. "Oh no, no, I know you would never. Of course not, I was just saying."

Once they're gone, I flop on the couch and try to find something to binge watch on Netflix. I'm debating between two different cooking competition shows when there's a knock on the door. I'm tempted to ignore it, but Rod and Carla specifically mentioned an important delivery I needed to sign for.

With a sigh, I head toward the door and look out the peephole. There's a courier with a package on his hip. He knocks again, and then checks his watch like maybe he knows I can see him and I'll get the point that he's got other packages to deliver. I crack the door open, the security chain still in place.

"Yeah?" I ask.

"Rod Mason?" he says, raising his eyebrows. I probably don't look like a Rodger. But I also don't feel like explaining, so I just nod.

"Package for you," he says, looking at me expectantly. It's a box, not an envelope he can slip through the crack to me. I groan a little, inwardly. I know it shouldn't be the first thing on my mind right now, but this guy is hot and right now I am...not. For the first time in a long time I reconsider my oversized sweats and t-shirt look.

I open the door and hold out my hands for the package, but he shakes his head. "Sorry, gotta sign."

I motion for him to follow me inside while I look around for a pen, and he does, closing the door behind him. I hear it click, and think to myself that's pretty ballsy of him, but when I turn around—pen up in the air like maybe I'll stab him with it—he's just standing in the front hall, smiling. I try to act like I wasn't going to impale him with a Bic as I take the clipboard from him.

"Now, remember to write Rod Mason, since it's not for you...Edie."

I glance up and he tips me a wink, a sly little one that almost has me smiling back until I realize something. "How do you know my name?"

"I know a lot of things, Edie," he says, voice calm. Like he's trying to keep me that way too. "Your name. Your Dad's name, the name of the thing that killed him."

"What?" I drop the clipboard and it clatters at my feet. "He was killed by a rogue wave."

The guy laughs. "No way. Leviathan doesn't have that

kind of power. Levi just hitched a ride on that wave, as a way to get to your father."

"Levi? Who the hell is that and why would he want to get to my father?"

The smile falters, the dimples disappear. "You really don't know, do you?"

I shake my head, and he drops the box. Whatever's inside crunches loudly in a way that tells me Rod and Carla's latest super delicate and expensive sculpture might be a little bit broken.

"Great," he says. "That's just...seriously?"

I edge away from him, back toward Carla's desk where I'm pretty sure there's a letter opener. I reach behind me, hands clattering over a calculator, her notebooks, and then —yes! The slim blade slips into my palm.

"Look," the guy goes on. "I'm the messenger god. Also, occasionally, a finder of lost things. Like you. But I didn't realize exactly how lost you would be. I figured your dad told his daughter—"

"Told me what?" I yell, brandishing the letter opener in front of me.

He studies me, and then he says, "Ichor."

The word stops me. It's the passcode Dad told me.

"Ichor," I repeat. "Blood of the gods."

"Aw, look at that. You do know things. Good job." He says it like someone praising an especially stupid little dog. "Yep, blood of the gods, and it's gonna get spilled real fast if we don't get you up to the Academy. I'm Hermes, by the way."

He holds out a hand, but I don't shake it, my fist still tight around the letter opener.

"Herpes?" I'm so confused.

He doesn't even blink. "One million two hundred thousand and seventy-eight."

"What?"

"That's how many times I've heard that joke. Now," he swipes the blade out of my hand—at least, I think he did. It's like he didn't even move. I just felt a breeze on my hand and then he had the letter opener...and I didn't.

"Listen," he says, tossing it back and forth. "I'm not going to hurt you. Obviously, your Dad didn't tell you much, but he did tell you the password."

"Ichor," I repeat, like maybe it'll protect me somehow from something. Like that Leviathan?

"Levi—Leviathan," I say aloud. "What is that? What killed my dad?"

Hermes walks over to an antique silk armchair that isn't actually meant for sitting. Or at least that's what I was told. But Hermes didn't get that message, apparently, because he collapses into it, still twirling the letter opener in his fingers. "Oh, Levi's nothing, really, just a water monster."

"A *monster*?"

"Not a particularly powerful one, either. Be glad they didn't send Scylla after him." He pauses. "But I guess they didn't have to. Levi got the job done."

"The job..." My heart, which has been like a rock in my chest, thumps hard, reminding me it's still there. "The job of killing my father, you mean?" And now I can feel the blood pumping through my veins too, and I realize as my hands start to tremble, that I'm not scared.

I'm pissed.

Hermes throws one leg over the side of Carla's chair, and that's when I spot them. Little wings on his feet, popping out of his ankle on either side.

"Holy shit," I say, backing away until the couch hits me in the knees. I fall onto it. "What is that? What are *you*?"

Hermes ignores me my order as he lifts up his leg.

"Didn't think wings would come as that much of a shock to you. Unless..." he cocks his head again, like he's getting messages from above. "You really don't know anything, do you?"

I shake my head. "Well you didn't know that I didn't know, so I guess we're both a little under-informed today."

He grins. "You're cute when you get feisty."

"Oh my god, are you seriously flirting with me right now?"

"Oh. My. *Me*. Yes I am." He tilts his head so his hair flops over his left eye. My mouth goes dry. He is so intensely...intense.

After six months spent with all my feelings on lock-down, it's too much. I pull out my inhaler and suck air into my too-tight lungs. By the time I tuck it away, I'm calm again.

I look back at Hermes, who is amusing himself with a sculpture of the Eiffel Tower made entirely of Barbie doll limbs. "I'd rather have the explanation without a side of flirtation."

He looks amused. "You think I can just turn all this charm on and off?"

"Yes."

"Okay, okay." He leans forward in the chair. "Have you ever had anything happen to you that you couldn't quite explain? And no—" He stops me before I can say, *yeah my dad being killed by a big water face*. "I mean something that happened to you, or maybe because of you? Something you did?"

I'm about to shake my head when I remember that first rush of water and the glass front doors of the condo going to pieces in front of me, the water rushing forward until...it stopped. But it didn't stop, it just kind of evaporated.

"Yes," I say. "Maybe."

"And what about..." Hermes gets up, moving slowly. "Don't think I'm being weird, kid. Just hold still, okay?"

I definitely think he's being weird and I keep a close eye on him as he circles behind me. He keeps telling me to relax and I keep telling him to back off, until finally he lets me have the letter opener back. I grip it tightly as he touches my back.

"I promise you can stab me if you think you need to," he says, and then his thumbs press down right between my shoulder blades and I scream.

It's a familiar pain, but one I haven't felt in a while. The school nurse had made one hell of a face when they did scoliosis checks in sixth grade, sending home a note saying that I probably need x-rays. Dad said I didn't, said the school should stick to worrying about test scores and he'd worry about his daughter's health. But then the pains began, and Mom developed a worry line between her eyebrows.

It had become a dull, constant ache, one that I carried with me every day and rarely notice anymore. Not until Hermes pushed on the spot. Immediately, one of my back spasms wracks me with pain.

"Don't touch me," I shout at Hermes, and I mean to sound tough, but it's useless. I just sound scared and hurt. And I dropped the knife, anyway.

"Sorry." He comes back around in front of me, face suddenly sympathetic. "You've never let them out?"

"Let what out?" I ask, still seething through the pain, though it's dulling.

He shakes his head. "Wow, that must hurt like a bitch. I feel like I've got fasciitis just after one day tucking mine in. Your father might've though he was protecting you, but really he wasn't doing you any favors."

"Don't you dare insult my dad," I tell him, my voice a little stronger.

"Okay, okay, look," he says, when he sees my frustration growing. "It's the easiest way to convince you. Listen to me. I want you to think about that pain, really feel it."

"I do feel it," I growl at him, rolling my shoulders.

"No, like *really* think about it. How it feels as if there's a center that it radiates from."

"Will doing this make the pain go away?"

"Make the pain go away? It'll be better than that. It'll be like the best morning stretch of your life."

An involuntary sigh whooshes from my lips at the thought of that sort of stretch. I close my eyes, re-thinking this ache that's been with me since sixth grade. "Two centers," I correct after a moment. "There's not just one."

"Great, good," he says. "Now I want you to focus on those centers with your mind and push them out."

I crack one eye open. "Push them *out*?"

"Yeah." He holds out his palms flat, moving his arms toward me. "Push that pain out, away from your body."

"Okay, weirdo," I say. Then I do.

The pain intensifies and I feel like I'm about to pass out, but then there's a release. It's so sudden and so complete that I drop to my knees.

There's a rush of wind past my ears, but there can't be. Carla and Rod keep all the windows shut tight for humidity control. I look through the doorway to my bedroom where the closet mirrors reflect my shock. That's not all they reflect.

Two leathery black wings sprout from my back.

6

"What the actual hell?" I ask.

I flex and the wings flex with me. That's it. I've lost my mind. As I stand and search for my phone, my wings clip two different sculptures. With a gasp, I spin around to grab them and hit two more.

I freeze, afraid of more destruction. "Make them go away."

"You need to practice shifting," Hermes tells me. "Then eventually you'll be able to change into a full"—he looks at me— "well, not sure what you are, honestly. Obviously you're not a werewolf, or a merfolk. I mean, we can rule out anything that doesn't have wings. Maybe you're a harpy. They're rare but not unheard of."

I hold up my hand to stop him. "How do I...un-wing?"

"You mean, shift back? Just think about pulling your power into yourself. I know that sounds weird but if you do it right, it won't hurt."

I concentrate. And nothing happens.

"You should partially shift at least once a day."

"Good to know." I rub my face. "Now what the hell is going on?"

"I'm here to invite you to attend Mount Olympus Academy."

"Oh my god," I say.

"Gods," he corrects.

I deflate. My dad is gone and my mom and sister are incognito. I pull into myself and feel kind of a pop. I turn around and around. My wings have disappeared!

My relief is short-lived. A quick look around tells that it was actually five different sculptures that smashed to the ground. Falling to my knees, I pick up pieces, wondering if there's any chance I can get them put back together.

"My foster people are going to kill me."

"Hmm." Hermes shrugs. "Humans murder over the strangest things."

I look up at him, unable to tell if he's joking. "I didn't mean literally."

He stands and holds out a hand. "Leave that junk. Leave these terrible people who have so much junk and come with me."

I stare at his hand, tempted for half an instant. Then shake my head and go back to sorting out lacquered gummy bears that had been shaped into a giant octopus.

"Look, I knew the password," he tells me. "Also, YOU SPROUTED WINGS. What more proof can I give you that the gods are real and you belong with them?"

"And you're here to take me to Hogwarts?"

"Mount Olympus Academy," he corrects with a gleam in his eye. "We'll help you, teach you about your past, and do our best to find your family."

"Find my family?" Gummy bears fall from suddenly numb fingers.

"Your mother and Mavis, right?"

I nod as tears suddenly threaten. "You could really find them?"

Hermes reaches down and lifts me to my feet. No— floats me to my feet. "For one of our students there is nothing we wouldn't do. Your mental and physical health is our first concern."

He seems sincere. There's a warmth in his eyes. And his hands which are still holding me. I want to smile back. I want to—

"Stop." I jerk away, breaking the contact and whatever he was doing to me. Almost like he was trying to hypnotize me with warm gooey niceness. "What was that? And what is this school really? You just want my organs, don't you? Are you going to sell my kidneys on the black market?"

Hermes has the audacity to laugh.

"Is this all just a joke to you?"

The laugher fades and he reaches out to me. I scuttle away.

He shakes his head. "I apologize. Okay? I didn't realize when I came here today that I'd have to explain everything to you. It's tedious and I thought a little charm might move us along a little faster." He pauses and frowns. "It's strange. It's been centuries since that little trick failed to work for me."

"Seduction is a *little trick*?"

He rolls his eyes. "Oh please. That wasn't seduction. If I wanted to seduce you, you would know."

Hermes takes another step toward me and though I want to hold my ground, I can't. I can't even hold his gaze, which is once again intense enough to make my breath short.

I pull out my inhaler and take a few short puffs before

I'm finally able to say, "I'm not going anywhere with you. I don't like you and I don't trust you."

"Not even for your mother and sister?"

"I. Don't. Trust. You," I repeat.

"Right." He nods. "And what about for your father?"

"He's dead."

"Yes. Murdered. And the ones responsible are laughing at how easy it was."

My hands clench into fists and my wings whoosh open once more.

Suddenly Hermes is at my side, not touching me, but his mouth so close to my ear I can feel his warm breath. "The Academy doesn't teach normal classes. We train creatures like yourself to hunt. We would teach you how to find those who killed your father. You could make them pay." He pauses and then adds softly. "For your grandmother too."

"Grandma?" My throat goes tight.

"That elevator falling was not an accident."

My heart is no longer a rock. It is solid and beating and furious. An hour ago it all seemed pointless. But suddenly I'm alive again. Dad and Grandma were taken from me and there was nothing I could do about it. Or so I thought. I can't turn back time. I can't bring them back. But maybe I can find justice.

Finally, I have a purpose.

I turn to look Hermes in the eye. "How soon can we leave?"

He smiles. "How quickly can you be ready?"

I run for my room, laughing as my wings catch more sculptures and they crash around me. It's less amusing when I can barely get down the hallway. Or through my bedroom door. Luckily, as I quickly throw some clothes into a satchel they fold up once more. I tear off my ripped t-shirt and study it for a moment, realizing my wardrobe is going to need some modifications if I'm gonna be doing that on the regular. Since I'm changing, I also switch out my dirty sweat-pants for jeans. The last thing I grab is Dad's cell phone. I gave up on trying to figure out the code to unlock it and haven't bothered to charge it.

Hermes calls from the other room, "You don't need to bring everything you own. You'll be given a uniform and anything else you need. Cell phones don't work on campus. Neither do computers. There's no WiFi, so nobody bothers. Bring some of that perfume you're wearing, though. It's got a nice smoky smell."

"Okay, creeper." I mutter, not bothering to inform him that I don't wear perfume. Quickly, I grab a few last things, like a framed picture of us just before summer. I've kept it face down on my bedside table. Now I look at it again.

Dad's mouth is open as he tells some joke I can't remember. The rest of us are laughing. We look so happy it hurts.

I shove the picture in my bag and go to find Hermes.

"Let's go. How did you get here? Do you have a car parked outside? If not, I have a bus pass."

Hermes grins. "Oh honey, I don't ride the bus."

"Well?" I ask.

"We're going to fly."

7

After ten minutes of trying to unravel my wings, Hermes gets frustrated and tells me to hop on his back. It's beyond awkward at first and I think we'll be too heavy for his little ankle wings, but he takes a running leap and we're airborne.

I cry out, but it's really not that scary. After everything I've been through, I mostly just feel exhilarated. I'm going to find Mom and Mavis. More importantly—I'm going to make whoever took my dad and grandma pay.

I look down on the beach-goers, still cleaning up. "Can't they see us?" I shout into Hermes' ear.

"What do you not get about god-magic?" he shouts back. Soon we're so high I can see way out into the water, the clouds just above us. Hermes flies inland, toward the swamps. I tighten my grip when he swoops.

"Follow the path of the lotus," he tells me. "You'll find the Academy."

"I don't understand..."

That's when Hermes drops me.

For the first few seconds all I can do is scream. As the

ground rushes toward me thoughts of my family fly through my mind. Reflex takes over and I feel the pain and release of my wings unfurling.

I hold them out and they catch the wind. My descent is softened. I let out a loud barking laugh. I can actually fly.

Well, I can fall less quickly. But still way too fast.

The ground—full of swamp trees and brackish water—comes up swiftly. I try to flap my wings but can't break my momentum.

I crash into the swamp.

I stand, shakily, drenched. The water is up to my knees. I will my wings to retract and am pleasantly surprised when they do. I am anything but happy about my surroundings, though. I'm in the middle of absolutely nowhere. The everglade bottom is slimy and unpleasant and I'll probably die of some weird fungal infection before I can even reach this mysterious academy.

"Thanks, Hermes," I shout up to the darkening sky. "You colossal asshole!!!"

Something slithers next to my leg in the water and I scurry to the nearest tree. All I can think about is Grandma's hatred of alligators. I hope I'm not about to become gator bait.

What did Hermes say? Follow the path of the lotus. What even is a lotus? I look around. In the distance is a light, and I figure it might be a camper--or some murdery swamp people—but hey, I don't have much of a choice at this point.

I walk for what feels like forever, smelly slime up to my knees, and sucking sound following me everywhere I go. And that's not all that's following me. There's definitely something in the trees. I can only hear it when I stop moving, but then it does, too, and I'm left staring suspiciously over my shoulder when I probably should be paying more attention to the water around me. Something sweeps past my legs and I jump, my wings accidentally sprouting. I swear I hear a giggle.

"Bite me," I say, then really wish I could take the words back. I have no idea what was in the water. I pull my wings back in, happy to note that it gets easier every time.

The light doesn't seem to be getting any closer, but the way starts to become easier and the water pulls at my legs, more like a river than a marsh. It smells better too; the heavy fecund scent of the wetland is replaced with a flowery perfume.

A flower actually floats by me, the current taking it ahead. A lotus is a flower! I remember and rush after it.

But rushing is hard in water, and the current changes direction suddenly, pushing against me rather than helping me along the way. I'll never get to that light if I don't think of something. The flowers are floating past me now in a torrent, seeming to tease me that it's so easy for them to get to where they're going.

"Hermes, I hate you," I tell him. I hate him for showing up in my life. I hate him for not telling me more. I hate him for coming onto me (and myself for liking it, just a little bit). But mostly I hate him for dropping me from the sky with no warning. Like a shitty parent just throwing a kid into the pool and telling them to swim.

Oh, wait. Maybe that's exactly what he was doing. Testing me.

Except I don't have to swim. I have to fly. There's only one problem with that.

"I DON'T KNOW HOW TO FLY!" I shout up at the sky. "I couldn't even pass a driver's test!"

No response.

"Fine," I say, and climb up on to the bank. Some lotus flower petals stick to my legs and I kick them off before popping my wings out.

I try flexing them. I get a couple inches off the ground, but not much. And I'm exhausted. I automatically reach for my inhaler. It's only once I bring it up to my mouth that I realize—I don't need it. I'm breathing hard, but I'm not breathless. My lungs aren't tight.

Having wings pop out of my back was crazy. But this is definitely the shock of the day. I look at the inhaler in my hand once more and then toss it over my shoulder, suddenly feeling free.

It's time to fly.

Birds, I tell myself. *Think about birds.*

But when I close my eyes I don't see little feathered birds. Two large beady eyes stare back at me. It should remind me of the alligators Grandma hated, but there is more intelligence in these eyes... and they're red. It's a deep, glowing red, like a ruby. No...like a ruby that's on fire. I stare back, entranced.

You are not a bird, those eyes tell me. *You are a force beyond nature. You are a—*

My eyes fly open. I don't want to hear more from whatever is inside of me staring out. It's too much. I've seen plenty of horror movies. Red eyes can't mean anything good.

I pull my wings back in, overwhelmed. And hopeless. I kneel beside the water to scoop some into my mouth, too thirsty to worry about it making me sick. What does it matter, I'll probably die out here. It's only as I dip my hands in that I notice the water has changed directions again. The flowers are moving towards the light.

What kind of river changes directions at will? I'm suspicious, but too tired to care as I slide back into the current, letting it take me toward the light.

One moment I'm thigh deep in water and the next I stumble through a rusty copper gate onto a grassy knoll.

Through a copse of trees I glimpse a gorgeous building. It looks like it's made out of white marble and belongs in Washington, DC more than a Florida swamp. Or... I realize. It belongs in Greece.

This must be Mount Olympus Academy.

"You have to find the way yourself, the first time," a voice at my shoulder tells me and I jump out of my skin. Literally. My wings unfurl. I'm starting to feel like a broken umbrella here.

"That's interesting." A girl in a private school uniform complete with Mary Jane shoes stands in front of me. I'm half embarrassed I look so shabby right now.

"I'm Cassie," she tells me with a toothy grin. "I saw we'd have a new student today. Also, the headmaster told me."

"I'm Edie," I tell her. "Who...I mean what..."

"Oh, I'm just your run of the mill seer. The witches and warlock crowd think I'm perfectly useless," she informs me cheerfully. "You, on the other hand." She reaches out and tugs at my wings.

"Hey!" I pull away. It has got to be rude to touch someone else's wings without asking.

"What *are* you?"

"I don't know. Hermes said I would learn in time."

"Well, let's get you sorted." she tells me. "First thing you have to choose your discipline so we know what dorm to place you into."

"Um yeah, hey Cassie, explain it to me as if I had no idea what you're talking about." I follow her, trying to get rid of my wings, but not succeeding. I just manage to hug them tightly against my body instead.

"Okay. Well, there are four different tracks. Defense is the least prestigious. That's where most of the witches and warlocks, including me, get sorted. But they bumped me last semester. They're all about healing, casting protective spells, or creating devices for those out in the fields."

"Sorta like Q does for James Bond," I say.

Cassie shrugs. "James Bond? Was he a student at your former academy?"

"No," I laugh. "James Bond is James Bond. He's fictional, or at least I think he is. The line between what's real and not feels pretty thin lately."

"I don't know what that means," Cassie says with a little gurgle of laughter. "But I think you're very funny."

We pass beneath a stone arch and enter a beautiful courtyard. An elaborate fountain sprays jets of water so high into the air that they disappear into the clouds.

"Wow," I can't help but say.

"What were we talking about again?" Cassie asks. She answers herself as I continue to gawk. "Oh right, the various disciplines. Next are the tracker and spy craft schools. They're separate but share a few of the same classes. It's also mostly shifters in those. You know, your run of the mill were-folk—you'd probably fit right in there." She tweaks the edge of my wing again and I jerk away.

"Hey, could you maybe not invade my personal space?"

Cassie's eyes grow wide. "Sorry!" Her hands fly up in surrender. "I'm terrible with boundaries. It's why the witches hate me. Well, they also say I don't know when to shut up. *And* I had a prophecy that half the class would cheat on the midterm exam and the professor overheard me when I announced it. So everyone sorta wants me dead—

not literally, I'm sure. Well, maybe literally." Cassie shrugs and looks sheepish. "But *we* could be friends. I mean, with those wings—" She very carefully gestures but doesn't touch. "You might be a bat. Not exactly the sexiest of shifters, but incredibly useful and great for tracking or spying."

Oh shit. With my luck I'm totally a bat. A flying rat.

I shouldn't be crushed, but I am.

Cassie, oblivious, continues talking. "And finally, the last and—let's be honest—most brutal of all the tracks, is the assassination class. A few of the less civilized shifters end up there, but it's mostly vampires. The violent ones love that track. Less thinking, more killing." Cassie makes little stabbing motions—I think. It's also possible she's trying to raise the roof. Finally her hand falls.

"I'm a little nervous, because that's where I'm going to be now. Midyear switch! After I got booted from defense the gods didn't know where to put me. They said I'd be useless as a spy since I can't shut up. And I'm a hopeless tracker; I barely know my left from my right. I think they figured if all else failed I could just talk our enemies to death. Honestly, I think expulsion would've been on the table if it wasn't for my mother working here. Thank goodness for the fact that this place wouldn't run without her."

"Is your mom the dean or something?" I ask.

"The Dean?" Cassie goggles at me like I've said something insane. "No, that's Mr. Zee. My mom runs the archives. She's a finder. Of objects and stuff, you know."

I nod, pretending like I do know.

"She started working here before I was born, so I was basically raised on campus. And since Mom's the only person who understands her filing system, they'll never be able to get rid of her." Cassie pauses and then adds with a little shrug, "Or me."

"Wow," I say. "You've never lived in the real world?"

"Nope. From what I've heard it's not that different from our world. Well, except for bathing in a huge tub of hot cocoa. I'd maybe like to go and try that out once."

I am debating whether or not to tell Cassie that is definitely not a thing, when suddenly her whole body goes rigid.

"Cassie?" I reach towards her as her eyes go milky white.

"You'll be in the assassination class too. We'll sit next to each other at lunch and share our meals. We'll be best friends." She blinks and her eyes are normal again. A giant smile spreads across her face. "Can you believe it? We're gonna be besties!"

Once again treading all over my personal space, Cassie throws her arms around me.

8

Cassie walks me straight to the admissions office, and takes a seat by the door. "Don't worry, Themis is always fair. She'll take good care of you. And I'll be right here when you're done."

"Great." I give her a thin smile and step inside.

A beautiful blonde woman sits behind the desk. She looks me up and down, pursing her lips. I feel super judged.

"Hello, Edie. Hermes told me he would be bringing you here today." She doesn't sound entirely happy about my arrival. Her long arm adjusts a pencil on her desk, putting it in line with all the other ones. "I'm the guidance counselor. You may call me Themis."

"Just Themis?" I ask. "Is that like your first name? Should I call you Miss Themis?"

She smiles faintly. "I'm no miss. If you must, Ms. Themis is fine, but our faculty doesn't depend on the use of honorifics to get the respect they deserve." She pauses a beat before adding, "Nor do I."

She stands and walks around her desk. "Please. Sit."

"I'll stand," I tell her. I've still got swamp water on me

and her furniture looks even nicer than the stuff Carla and Rod had. Plus, I'm too weak to pull my wings in. I tried earlier, and they just drooped there.

She nods and studies me, arms crossed. "I'm sure Cassie filled you in on our various disciplines. That girl isn't good at much, but she certainly can talk."

"That's mean," I tell her.

Ms. Themis smiles wanly. "Sometimes the things I say may sound...harsh, but it's in my nature to judge. And to create order. Please, let me help you."

She puts a hand on my shoulder and my wings are suddenly gone. "You'll get better at this, don't worry," she tells me kindly. "Now sit so we can chat."

I collapse tiredly into the chair and she returns to her side of the desk. "What did Cassie tell you about our Academy?"

"There are...were-people and vampires...and..." I stop. It's all a jumble in my mind.

"We help people like you. People who shift into other shapes. People who don't belong anywhere else. We train them as protectors, or as spies, or sometimes they track down dangerous monsters. And sometimes they kill them."

I sit up.

"That's it. I want to kill monsters," I tell her.

"Shifters mostly become spies. Depending on what they shift into. That discipline would be most beneficial to you—"

I shake my head. "A monster murdered my family. I want to become..." I think about what Cassie told me. "I want to become an assassin."

Ms. Themis' lips twitch. "The assassination class is the most rigorous. And you're coming to us late in the year." She pauses then asks. "What kind of student were you at your previous schools?"

"Really good," I lie.

"I do have your records," Themis replies with one single perfectly raised eyebrow.

"Oooh." I quickly backtrack. "I meant I was always on time and attentive and..." I wrack my brain for another positive and can only come up with, "clean."

"Impressive."

I can feel myself being pushed away from the assassin track which is my only reason for being here. And that is not happening. "Look, I don't test well. It's a high pressure situation—"

Themis breaks in. "All our classes are high pressure. Especially the assassination class ones." There is something like pity in her eyes and I can feel her gearing up for the part where she lets me down gently.

"Wait! Cassie had a vision—that's what she does, right? Predict the future? She saw us in the assassination class together."

"Cassie's visions are not set in stone. Quite the opposite, really. The future can be changed. Cassie also sometimes exaggerates what she sees."

I stand. "Look, I came here for one thing. I'm not going to waste my time spying on whoever." I take a deep breath and attempt to stare down a god. "I. Want. Revenge."

Ms. Themis nods slowly. "That's easy to say, Edie, but I don't think you fully appreciate the gravity of the situation."

"My father was killed. I understand the gravity just fine."

"He was killed. But you must understand that it wasn't a random act of violence. Your father was a casualty of war. A war that we've been fighting for much longer than you've been alive. The other side has one goal: the complete eradication of the gods who run this Academy as well as anyone we've trained or worked with. They will not stop until everything and everyone we love is destroyed."

War. It's a heavy little word. For some reason I'd had the idea that this was more of a rival gang situation. The wave monster guy versus the gods. But war is way bigger. And messier. Yet somehow I'm now in the middle of one and volunteering—no, insisting—on fighting.

It occurs to me that I might be in over my head. I gulp and resist the urge to run out of the room screaming.

"Who exactly are these people we're at war with?"

"They're not people at all. They're monsters."

"Ummm..." I hesitate because I'm pretty sure this is a stupid question. But still, it's gotta be asked. "You mean *literally*? Actual monsters, like that Levi thing that murdered my father?"

"Yes, indeed. They are monsters in all senses of the word. The students in our assassination class are trained to meet them on the battlefield—wherever that may be. Though it pains me to admit it, these students must in some ways become every bit as monstrous as those they are fighting." She pauses and levels me with a hard gaze. "You need to ask yourself if you truly are up to this challenge. You haven't been raised with this knowledge. However hard everyone else works, you will have to work twice as hard. You'll have to take the full load of assassination classes, as well as a remedial flying class so that you can learn how to use your wings. Are you ready for this?"

For six months I've done nothing but grieve and mope and be sad. My father and grandmother are dead. Murdered. My sister and mom are missing. Maybe dead too. I am for all purposes completely alone in the world.

I close my eyes and the giant glowing ones from the

swamp once again stare back at me. Maybe I'm not completely alone after all. Whatever I'm meant to shift into is inside me...and apparently it has opinions too. Or one opinion, at least. It wants to be in the assassination class. The idea of war doesn't scare it one bit. The eyes communicate that as clearly as any written message might. They are glittering. And eager. And ready.

My wings are not a broken umbrella. They are this thing inside of me, struggling to come out.

I am terrified.

But also, weirdly sorta...excited?

"Yeah," I say. I stand and my wings burst out of my back and billow into the room. "I am ready for this."

I didn't understand how exhausted I was until I lay down on my bed. Almost immediately I am dead asleep. It seems like only seconds later I'm being shaken awake.

"Who are you and what are you doing in my bed?" A girl dressed all in black stands over me, daggers in her gaze.

I blink blearily. "Your bed?" I look around.

"Yeah, dummy. My bed. If you're my new roommate obviously your bed is the one with all the new stuff on it."

I scramble to my feet. "Sorry. I didn't realize."

"Whatever. I heard about you," she tells me, tearing the blanket and sheets off her bed, like I have some kind of contagious disease.

Already? I think. I imagine Cassie, bursting at the seams with news, running off to tell everyone about my arrival.

"You're the shifter who thinks she's something special," the girl continues.

That definitely doesn't sound like something Cassie would say. No, I'm guessing my new roomie added that part all on her own. We're definitely not going to be having pillow fights anytime soon, or painting each other's nails.

She lies on her stripped bed. "Well, you're *not* special. I give you two weeks before you fail out. Or are dead." She smirks at this last bit. Like she's imagining it and likes what she sees.

"Well, nice to meet you too," I tell her. "I'm so glad my roommate is a supportive person and not a soul sucking bitch."

Her eyes flick to me. "Blood sucking bitch."

"Whaaaa?"

She makes a hissing noise and flashes me her fangs.

Oh. Hell. No.

"Don't worry, I'd rather eat roadkill then suck on a shifter."

"Super comforting," I mumble, turning to my bed and all the stuff covering it.

There are clothes—new underwear and pajamas and my uniforms. Ms. Themis said that the uniforms are magic and when I shift will allow space for my wings. Other than that the uniform looks like pretty standard private school stuff, complete with knee high socks and a preppy tie.

Also in the pile are books, and on top is my class schedule. ASS CLASS is printed in block letters at the very top and I let out a laugh. My roommate eyes me.

"You know, I may not sleep but I do like quiet."

"I was just...ass class..." I giggle. "I'm Edie, by the way."

She huffs. "I'm Valentina. My friends call me Tina."

"Nice to meet you, Tina," I say sarcastically.

"I said my *friends* call me Tina. You are definitely not one of my friends, so let's not do this."

"Do what?" I ask.

She turns. "This roomie thing. You and I are not going to

ever *be* friends. I am going to pretend that you don't exist and try very hard not to kill you, since that will get me kicked out of the Academy. You are going to try and stay out of my way."

"But..."

"Let me explain something to you. This is the warmest welcome you're going to get. No one in the assassination class is going to think your little wide-eyed 'gee shucks' act is cute. That kind of bullshit could get us all killed." Tina turns away from me. "The less you talk, the better for your health."

I take a deep breath. Ass Class? More like Asshole Class. I turn my back on my less-than-friendly new roomie.

"Oh, and don't touch my Vee."

"What?" I whirl back around. "Don't touch your *what*?"

Tina smiles, obviously thrilled at the reaction. "Vee, my Venus Fly Trap," she says, and points to the corner, where a huge plant rests by the window.

"Um, is that breathing?" I ask.

"No," Tina tosses her hair. "But I wouldn't be surprised at all if Vee became self-aware one day. You're a terribly smart little angiosperm, aren't you?"

Her voice merges into baby talk on the last sentence, and she actually scratches the plant under the chin. I swear, it smiles. I can see myself waking up in the morning missing a finger, and Vee slowly digesting her breakfast.

Feeling deflated and realizing that Cassie might be the exception rather than the rule as far as friendliness goes, I spend some time sorting through my new stuff before making my bed and crawling under the covers. I take the picture of my family and place it on my nightstand, feeling very alone.

You'd think it would be impossible for me to fall asleep

with a real-life blood-thirsty vampire laying a few feet away, but when I close my eyes, the glowing eyes blink back at me. It's almost as if they're trying to tell me they'll keep watch while I sleep. And even though it's ridiculous, it's comforting too. I sink into a deep sleep.

9

I wake in the morning to find Tina levitating a few inches above her bed, reading. I think Vee might have turned her head a little, like the plant is reading over her shoulder. Hmmm, if vamps don't sleep they have a whole eight extra hours to study. How will I ever keep up with them?

I realize I am thoroughly screwed.

Great start to the day.

I also realize that, despite the venom of her words, she was right about one thing she said last night. I can't go googly-eyed every time something weird happens. Weird shit is my new normal.

I turn my shocked wide-open mouth into a yawn and sit up to stretch. Tina thumps down on her bed, shoots me a look promising retribution, and then quickly gets to her feet. Like, she doesn't just get up, she literally goes from horizontal to vertical like an old-timey Dracula movie.

"I'm going to use the bathroom. I have a daily routine that I'm not interrupting for you. If you can't hold it maybe we can put some newspaper in the corner for next time." With an evil laugh she disappears into the bathroom.

Instead of thinking about how badly I need to pee, I get dressed. I'm more than a little disconcerted that the sexy Catholic school girl look kind of works for me. I check myself out in the mirror, testing my wings while Tina spends FOREVER in the bathroom. Does a vampire even *use* the bathroom? I snicker at the thought.

I decide to distract myself with trying to get my wings under control.

That's because another thing Tina said last night has been bothering me. If everyone already thinks I'm a joke, I can't have my wings popping in and out all through class.

Now I take a deep breath and push. My wings pop out of my uniform and I'm surprised to see they're an iridescent blue.

"Are they supposed to change colors?" I ask my reflection.

Tina finally comes out of our bathroom.

"Are you a show girl or something? Planning to hit the Vegas strip?" she says, eyeing my wings.

"They're blue," I say.

"Oh, good job on color identification," she says. "We can bump you right up out of the toddler classes now."

"Bite me," I say, then quickly follow that up with, "Wait, no don't."

I'm alarmed to see that Tina's fangs have come out, but she covers them with her lip. "Don't invite me. Seriously," she says. "I'm not getting kicked out over your trashy mood-winged ass."

"Mood? Is that what it is?" I turn checking out my wings from behind. They're a pretty sort of blue right now, a little metallic sheen to them.

"Or maybe they just trying to compensate for that lame uniform," Tina says with a little laugh.

"Um, you have to wear the same uniform."

She holds out her arms, displaying her super punk look. Ripped black tights paired with big black stomper boots. Safety pins are fastened down the length of her skirt and her white shirt is unbuttoned revealing an old Metallica t-shirt that hangs off one bony shoulder.

I hate to admit it, but she looks super-hot.

"Aren't there uniform regulations?" I ask, eyeing my own perfectly preppy uniform in the mirror.

"Vamps don't follow regulations, Swamper." She stops in front of the mirror and smooths back a few stray hairs. I can't resist peeking to see if there's a reflection there. Catching my eye in the mirror she smirks, letting me know that she knows exactly what I'm doing.

"Swamper?" I ask. I can tell by the tone that what she just called me is not good, but I have no idea what it means.

"Yeah," she checks her reflection one more time. "You're a total Swamper. You might have made it through the gates physically, but mentally you're still out in that swamp. You don't belong here, period."

She does one last adjustment, pinching a lock of hair between her fingers and pulling downwards. It turns green under her touch, an eye-catching little highlight. Tina catches me watching and drops the strand fast. She clears her throat and shrugs into a backpack, finally turning to look at me.

"That blue looks pretty hopeful. Optimistic, even," Tina says. "That's gonna change fast."

On that note, she leaves, not offering to show me around campus or help me find my first class. Which, printed at the top of my schedule, appears to be something called, "Killing with Your Bare Hands."

Since I'm coming in almost halfway through the year I

must be really far behind. Some of the shine comes off my wings, telling me they are definitely mood related. I tuck them back inside my skin as my stomach rumbles, reminding me I don't know where the cafeteria is, either.

Luckily, I don't need to worry about finding my way around campus. Cassie is parked outside my door, greeting me with a huge smile and an offer to take me to the dining hall for a quick breakfast, followed by Killing with Your Bare Hands, and then my next class, and the one after that.

"We have the same schedule," she tells me, practically glowing. "Well, except for remedial flying, obviously. I can't fly."

"Me neither," I mutter.

"You'll be with me practically all day, every day!" Cassie says, spinning.

"Hooray," I say, half-meaning it. Her enthusiasm is exhausting, and it's not even nine a.m. She's obviously not the coolest kid on campus. Not that I was ever into chasing after popularity. I used to be happy with my middle of the pack social group. I would've said we were pretty welcoming to everyone. That is, until they dropped me after the supposed gonorrhea incident. It sucks to be at the bottom of the food chain.

The way Cassie waves to other students, calling out their names while they nod back coolly or ignore her entirely, tells me it's even worse than I thought. Cassie isn't just uncool. She's social kryptonite. At my old school she'd be the girl your mom *made* you hang out with because she felt sorry for her. On the other hand, she hasn't threatened to kill me yet, which was Tina's way of saying hello.

I glance at my schedule again, as my stomach growls. Nobody even asked if I was hungry when I showed up yesterday.

"I wonder what's for breakfast?" I say aloud, and Cassie's eyes immediately roll back into her head, the whites glowing and her face going slack.

"Seven grain waffles. Steak and eggs, extra rare," she intones in a deeply creepy voice. "Blood and yogurt parfaits."

Her eyes roll forward once more and she gives me a cheery smile. "Oops! Sorry. I know my prophecies are annoying. They're always about, like, if it'll rain on Wednesday or who has a foot fungus. Nobody really listens to me anymore."

She says it like it's funny, and not incredibly depressing.

It does end up being helpful, though, to know to avoid the parfaits as we go through the breakfast line. I might've thought it was some sort of strawberry syrup without the forewarning.

Killing With Your Bare Hands is in a room that is half classroom, half gym. Cassie and I take a seat near the back while the other students seem to already have their cliques. Of course, it is halfway through the term. Tina is surrounded by a whole gaggle of girls with resting bitch face.

The class is taught by an extremely tall, very hot, very shirtless man who introduces herself as Kratos.

I turn to Cassie and jerk my head in the teacher's direction. "Mr. Kratos?"

"Drop the Mr. He's just Kratos."

"Okay, but Kratos...he's a god, right?"

"Demi-god, technically," she whispers back. "Of war." Her eyes widen dramatically, like she finds this both scary and exciting.

I guess that also sums up how I feel about this dude—er, god. I can't seem to rip my gaze away from his bare torso.

Golden skin covers bulging muscles. So. Many. Muscles. He is definitely a badass. He has it written all over himself. Like literally. It's tattooed across his back.

He sidles past my desk, giving me a little smirk to let me know he saw me checking him out. Then he tells us to open our books to page three hundred and five. It's a chapter titled, "They're Not Actually Dead Until They Piss Themselves."

"Alright, who wants to walk us through strangulation?" Kratos asks.

Almost everyone immediately raises their hands. Great, so not only is this the most difficult course, but it's full of overeager super achievers. Kratos skims over the extended arms and then does the classic teacher thing of picking a guy at the back who seems more interested in studying the ceiling.

"Val," Kratos nods to him. "Please come to the front of the classroom."

The boy stands and for the first time I miss my inhaler. This school is overrun with extremely good-looking people, but there's something about Val that's more than just pretty. He walks to the front, all liquid and smooth, like he's not made out of flesh and bone. I realize pretty quickly he might not be. I have to remember I'm not in high school anymore —I'm at Mount Olympus Academy. He's got his uniform a little bit punked out, like my roommate Tina, but he's wearing a t-shirt with a cute bunny rabbit under it, which feels very not-vampire to me.

"What is he?" I whisper to Cassie.

"And for your victim," a hand settles onto my shoulder, heavy and squeezing more than necessary. "The new girl, who likes to talk during class."

Everyone giggles. Even Cassie, although I'm starting to

realize it's her auto-response to everything. Kratos propels me to the front of the class, while I fight the urge to adjust the back of my skirt and make sure I didn't tuck it into my underwear when I used the bathroom.

"Hi," I say to Val when I get up to him, and he nods, using the motion to both acknowledge me and toss a shiny black curl out of his eyes.

"Hey," he responds, his voice low and slightly rumbly. The last thing I need is some dumb crush—especially after my last one ended so badly. And yet with just that one word I can feel the fascination forming. My eyes latch onto his shirt, which is a sunny yellow. This close, I can read the words printed above the trembling rabbit, which say, *Inside I'm just a scared wittle bunny wabbit.*

"Your shirt is great," I say, nervously.

"I know," he agrees in a way that is both dickish and inexplicably attractive. I frown as the shivers travel down my spine. I refuse to fall under this guy's spell. And that means no more sweet little Edie. I'm in the assassination class now. I need to be a badass.

"Not that you care, but I'm Edie." Okay, that was more passive aggressive than badass. I'll have to keep working on it.

"No," Val replies with another hair flip. "You're dead."

And then I'm in the air—not because my wings are out, but because Val's got my neck in one hand.

10

I automatically grab Val's wrist and pull, but it's like steel. I look down into his bright blue eyes, silently begging him to stop because I don't have the ability to speak right now.

He doesn't, and Kratos begins to narrate my death.

"You can see by the way her color is changing that the oxygen has been cut off. First the skin will go gray—"

At their desks, students lean in closer, taking notes on my skin tone. Tina is in my line of vision and her gleeful smirk enrages me. My lungs are on fire, black spots popping in my vision. I claw and scratch at Val's hands, but I'm not even leaving marks on his skin. My vision begins to darken and my chin slumps onto my chest.

I'm about to pass out. My eyes flutter closed. Suddenly the eyes of the thing inside me stare back. They are angry. And they remind me that I'm not completely defenseless.

My wings pop. I open my eyes and glimpse them in my peripheral vision. They are lustrous and bright red with anger. The sight of them gives me strength. I give a gigantic *push*, both wings wafting around me, creating a draft that makes Val unclench his fist and sends him sprawling back onto his ass.

There's a gasp from the whole class as I settle back onto the ground, and I don't know why. Surely on a campus full of vampires and werewolves, a girl with wings is not a big deal? But people aren't looking at my wings. They're looking at Val—who is on fire.

"Oh shit," I yell, but Kratos is already on it, casting a heavy blanket over Val and rolling him across the floor until he's just a tube of cloth, with feet sticking out the bottom and hair out of the top. Singed, smoking hair.

"I'm so sorry," I say, running up to Kratos, who gives me a shove that sends me rolling down the aisle.

"Don't approach without permission," he shouts, casually flipping the blanketed Val into the air, unrolling him. He hits the ground, blackened skin smoking. There are only scraps left of his t-shirt that I'd admired a few moments ago. His perfect face is still perfect, but the rest of him...

He's ruined. He's dying. The skin on his chest is peeling away, revealing white bones beneath.

And somehow, I did that.

Tina stands over Val, trembling. "What did you do to him?"

I'm crying, or at least I think I am. The tears are evaporating on my cheeks, sending steam into my eyes.

"I'm so, so sorry," I keep saying over and over again as I kneel next to Val. I look up at Kratos, who is standing dispassionately over us.

"Fern! We need a medic over here!" Kratos calls and a girl who was standing off to the side of the class rushes over, a bag at her side.

She pulls a metal thermos from the bag and gives Val a drink of whatever is inside. His skin stops bubbling and his eyes flutter open. The open skin closes back up. But it's still black and ugly. Like a burnt piece of paper. He looks like he could easily crumble.

"Finish fixing him," Tina screeches. She picks the medic up with one hand and gives her a little shake.

"That's enough," Kratos says, easily removing the shaking medic from Tina's grasp. "Remember this young witch is also in training. She did what she could, but Val will need a trip to the infirmary to finish healing."

Even as he says the words, two older medics bustle in with a stretcher between them.

As they lift Val, his mouth goes back to its normal position—but not before I spot his elongated fangs. He's a vampire.

"He's fine," Kratos says. "Burns can be tricky but vampires naturally defy most injuries. Fire is the most difficult for them, though. Good thinking, new girl."

"Yes, good thinking, Swamper," Tina echoes, her ire focused on me once more as the young medic exits with Val. "If this were a defense class."

"What was I supposed to do?" I ask. "Just die?"

"No," Kratos says. "But Tina has a point. This was a demonstration. I assumed you were a vampire, because you are rather attractive. That was my mistake. I should have known your limitations."

"She's wearing a regulation uniform," Cassie argues. "You should've known she wasn't a vamp."

Kratos only shrugs. "Human clothes don't interest me."

"Awesome," I mutter. "I almost died because you didn't do your research."

"No," Tina is quick to counter. "Valentino almost died. My brother better be okay or you'll only *wish* you were dead."

"You're…" Almost immediately my brain makes the connection between Valentino and Valentina. Yep, those are definitely twin names. Terrible twin names, but twin names just the same. "Oh."

Tina turns to the class, hands on her hips. "I demand to know what she is. These classes require a certain amount of trust. They make all of us vampires take blood oaths, disclosing any extrasensory abilities. But this one just waltzed in here, a complete unknown. Did we learn nothing from the incident last semester? I think I speak for all of us when I say that we can't trust this Swamper, this *thing*, when we don't even know what she is."

I wait for the teacher or Cassie or someone to defend me. Instead there are head nods all around and even some scattered applause.

Kratos turns to me and even before he speaks I have an idea of what he's going to say. "That's fair. And Tina makes good points." He frowns, thinking. "Also, you breathed fire and that's not something we've seen—ever." Kratos tilts his head up toward the ceiling, the same way Hermes did back at the foster's house. "This is above my pay grade," he tells it. He waits a moment, seeming to listen, before focusing his attention back on me.

"Themis wants to see you. Says she'll straighten this all out."

Tina smiles, making it clear her fangs are out. "That's all I wanted, sir."

I remember Cassie saying Themis was a stickler for the rules. Was there one against burning your classmate? And if so, what is the punishment?

"Now?" I ask Kratos.

He nods.

I gulp. I guess I'm about to find out.

11

"Twenty minutes into your first class and you're back in my office." Ms. Themis glares over the top of her glasses. "I'm afraid this does not bode well for your future at Mount Olympus Academy."

"What are you saying? Am I getting expelled on my first day?" I sink further into my chair.

"Don't get ahead of yourself. Expulsion would be a last resort. And Mr. Zee would make that decision, not me. However, this may be a sign that the assassination class is simply..." she pauses and shoots me an apologetic look. "Not a good fit."

She's right. I know she's right. And yet, "I thought he was killing me. It didn't feel like an exercise. Also if that had been real, I would've won. Isn't it good that I didn't freeze up? You said we're at war. Don't you need someone who does what needs to be done? I honestly didn't know if I could kill someone, but now...now I think I could." It's a strong speech, despite my wavering voice.

But Themis is unimpressed. "We need more than beings capable of killing. I would call that the bare minimum requirement, actually." She stands and comes around the front of the desk. "I don't suppose Cassie told you about the incident we dealt with over summer semester?"

I shake my head, confused by the sudden change of subject.

"We lost a student in battle. At first we feared it was two, but one played dead, and though badly wounded, managed to make her way back to us. We were so relieved at having this student returned that we never questioned her story. It never occurred to us that she might've been compromised. Months passed before we realized she'd been turned and had become an agent working with the monsters—against us. With the help of another student, she escaped before we could fully interrogate her."

Themis slams the desk with a balled up fist. Then she gestures to the golden scale sitting on the far edge of the table. Nothing sits on either end of the scale and yet the one side floats higher than the other. "Ever since then the scales have been unbalanced. The whole campus is on edge. Trust has been frayed." Her hand closes around my jaw, forcing my eyes up to meet her own. "And the war—we are closer to losing everything than we ever have been before. The Academy was always a sacred place, free of fear, but now that it's been invaded once, it will never be the same again. The next time the war comes here it will not slip through the gates in disguise, but instead tear them right down. If the scales are to be tipped the other way, in our favor, we will need to be strong. A chain is only as strong as its weakest link."

I stare at her. "And right now, I'm the weak link?"

"I honestly don't know. You're strong, with an unknown power. You must understand, though, everyone here is strong. We need more than that. We need a team that works together. Seamlessly. Doubtlessly."

She releases me and returns to her side of the desk. I rub where her fingers dug into my skin. "I understand that," I say quietly. "And I want to be part of that team."

"Then it's time to shift, so we can all see what's on the other side of your skin."

She makes it sound like I'm a shirt that's on inside out. "I don't know how."

"Take that." Ms. Themis points at her desk, to a glowing lump of something that looks like mold. Hesitantly, I reach forward and take it in my hands. I'd expect it to be slimy, but it's hard and smooth as a rock. "Hold the stone between both hands. Close your eyes. And just breathe."

I do as she instructs. The moment my eyes close, the thing inside me stares back. It snorts anxiously and steam rises, hot enough to warm my face. It wants out. But it—me —is also scared. As searing pain rips through me, I realize why.

"Auuughh!" The scream rips from my throat.

My eyes fly open. Dropping the stone, I leap to my feet. "What the hell, lady?"

She nods, calm as ever. "As I suspected. Your shifter self is trapped inside of you. A magic spell that was no doubt made to last a lifetime. Your father's work, I'm betting. No doubt he was trying to protect you."

"My *Dad* cast a spell on me? I don't think so. He didn't like brushing my hair because I'd scream when she'd tug too hard."

"But this would have been painless. And your father was quite talented in the magical arts."

"We are both talking about Danny Evans, right?"

This earns me a small smile. "We are indeed. But your

father wouldn't have shackled your shifter self without having some release mechanism."

"Release mechanism? Don't even think of telling me to bend over and cough. Not after that stone—" I hold out my hands which have been stinging horribly and for the first time I notice they're covered in angry red blisters. "Holy shit!"

"Yes, you'll need to visit the infirmary before your next class." She consults the watch on her wrist. "And you ought to hurry. Being late will not help your situation."

Relief pours through me. "So I'm still in the assassination class?"

"For now. But"—Ms. Themis holds up one long finger—"you must let go of the fear and find a way to free your inner...whatever it is inside you, or I will have no choice but to find another place for you."

The infirmary is the next building over, which makes it easy to find. Fern, the medic who helped Val, is there. I expect her to be stand-offish but she waves me over.

"That was an impressive display in class," she says to me with a lopsided grin. "I've never seen anyone take down a vamp like that."

"Totally not on purpose," I tell her.

"You'll learn to control it...whatever it is." She takes out a bottle and squirts it on my tender skin. It stings a bit as it foams. "It seems hard now, but you'll get through."

"Thanks." I say, weirdly touched by her kindness.

"Us girls with little old lady names have to stick together," she tells me, flashing her broad smile. She wipes the foamy medicine off my arm. My skin is as good as new. It's absolutely amazing.

Well, amazing to me. I can't help exclaim, "Like magic!"

Fern lets out a little laugh. "That's because it *is* magic."

"Oh. Right."

Fern leaves me to attend another student and I eye the magic medicine. I hesitate a moment and then shove the can of the spray foam into my bag. With a vampire for a roommate it seems like it might be a handy thing to have.

A glance at the clock tells me I only have ten minutes before my next class starts. Throwing my bag over my shoulder, and with a farewell wave to Fern, I rush from the room and almost immediately slam into a wall of cold steel muscle. I reel backwards and stumble over my own feet. Before I can land on my ass, the wall grabs hold of me, reeling me back in.

Of course, it's not a wall. It's a bare chest. Less extravagantly muscled than Kratos, and smoother, but still undeniably masculine.

"Oh," I say. "I'm sorry, I—" I finally stop ogling the perfect chest and move my gaze upwards to an equally perfect face. A perfect face I already know too well. "Val."

"Edie. Right?" He smiles, his pointy canines not at all threatening. At least that's what I tell myself.

"I'm really, really sorry for burning you. I mean you look good now—" My eyes can't help but drift back down to his bare torso. "Really good." Quickly I refocus while I can feel my face burning red with embarrassment. He lifts his eyebrows slightly as if to say he knows exactly why I'm blushing and then returns the favor, his eyes sweeping down my body and back up again.

"You look good too," he says at last.

I can't tell if he's mocking me or if he's sincere, or maybe some combination of both.

"That reminds me, your t-shirt. It was ruined."

He shrugs. "No biggie. Tina made it for me. I've got several others like it. It's a joke between us. She says I'm the least discriminating vampire in the world when it comes to fashion." He pauses and then adds with a smile private smile. "And other things too."

I want to ask what those other things are, but it feels too forward. "I should go. I've got class." I spin around and make a lunge for the door, suddenly desperate to exit this awkward conversation before I make a total fool of myself.

"Me too. I'll walk with you." Val reaches for the door handle a split second before me so that my hand lands on top of his. His hand, like his chest, is cool to the touch.

"Great!" I say, forcing myself to let go.

We walk in silence as all around us students pour from different buildings and out across the quad. There's no missing the way people stare at me, or the double takes when they see Val at my side.

"Is this a deliberate display?" I ask him. "Showing everyone there's no hard feelings?" "There *aren't* any hard feelings. You're an animal." I visibly bristle at this, but Val shrugs. "All shifters are animals. You felt threatened and acted on instinct."

"I *was* threatened. You nearly killed me."

"I smelled that you were human. I would've stopped," Val says, and then adds with an arch smile, "before you set me on fire."

"I'm..." I'm close to saying I'm sorry again, but since it appears I didn't actually damage Val, I'm not feeling nearly as bad as I did before. Plus, I'm not entirely sure I believe him.

We enter a shady path that runs between two of the buildings and Val suddenly stops. "At least tell me it was special for you. You don't set every guy you meet on fire, do you?"

He's flirting with me. Not just flirting. He's looking down at me with that heavy lidded look like he's thinking of kissing me. Which is crazy! The medics might have healed his body, but they couldn't quite remove that burnt flesh smell from what was left of his clothes and hair. He needs a good long shower—maybe two—before that will be washed away.

And yet, he leans in closer.

"Who else have you set on fire, little Edie?" His voice is teasing. Coaxing. Like this is all just a joke.

"No one," I start to say, but then with a gasp I remember. "Oooh, so it really wasn't gonorrhea."

As the sexy look disappears from Val's face, I realize I've said that last bit aloud.

"No! I don't have...I didn't give, or get...or transmit." Stopping, I take a deep breath. "I made out with a boy at school. It was, you know, fine."

"Fine?" Val is back to being amused, and slightly flirtatious. Though more cautiously so.

"Well, there were some other things going on like he had a girlfriend and I—*we* shouldn't have been kissing, but that's not important to this story. The crucial bit is that he had a rash at school the next day and told everyone I'd given him gonorrhea."

Val's lip curls. "Humans are disgusting."

"Well yeah, I mean, this human was. But anyway, I figured it was some sort of reaction to my soap or moisturizer. Now, though, I think, is it possible that I..."

"Burned him?" Val helpfully finishes for me. He rubs his chin as he thinks about this, playing at thoughtfulness. "I'd guess it was more likely that you when you got hot and bothered, this boy ended up slightly singed."

I slap a hand over my mouth and then moan from behind it. "I'll never be able to kiss anyone again."

Val, the jerk, has the audacity to laugh at this.

"Oh, I'm so glad you're amused," I huff.

"Edie..." He reaches for my hands and I jerk them away. "We're gonna be late for class."

He catches hold of my hand, refusing to let me push past him. "No we won't. It's right around the corner." I tug at our joined hands but he refuses to release me. "What are you, Edie? I've never seen anyone create fire before. Not from their mouths, anyway."

"That does seem to be the question of the day." I try to make it a joke, but my voice wobbles toward the end. Frustrated, I fling myself back just as Val finally lets me go. I stumble several steps and as I blink Val is suddenly there to catch me. It seems impossible that he could move so fast. But lots of things seem impossible these days.

"Can I..." He hesitates as he sets me back on my feet and then takes a step back. "Can I see your wings again? I was a little on fire the last time so it was difficult to get the full picture. The guys pushing my gurney to the infirmary gushed the whole way there about how extraordinary they were."

There is something about the way he says it, totally sincere with not even the slightest hint of his usual underlying mockery, that I can't resist. I set my backpack on the ground and then like a girl doing a twirl in a pretty dress, I fan my wings out. And then am embarrassed when I realize they are a rosy blushing pink.

"Nice," he says, reaching out to run a finger along my wing. It's a gentle touch, slow and soft. The wings twitch and send a shiver down my spine. And I don't mind it... at all. "Now I see why they've been looking for you."

"Huh? Who's been looking for me?"

At that moment a bell begins to toll.

"Uh-oh, that's our cue that class is about to start."

"About to start? You said we had time!"

"No, I said it was right around the corner. And it is. Which is why we have time for this." Leaning forward he presses his lips to my cheek, just barely catching the corner of my mouth. "You'll kiss again," he says softly as he pulls away. "You just need to find the right person."

And then before I can react or reply, he grabs my hand and tugs me through the corridor and out into the sunlight where the rest of our class is already waiting. Depositing me beside Cassie, he drifts off into the crowd of vampires. It's almost like he was never there at all.

Except when I touch the spot where he kissed me, it's still cold to the touch.

12

Me almost dying pretty much sets the routine for the next few weeks.

I try to keep my head down but Cassie and I are the only non-vamps in the Ass Class, so we kind of stick out. I thought things might be easier in Tracking for Assassins, since it's an interdisciplinary class. The trackers are mostly shifters, so it seemed possible that I might actually make some friends.

I thought wrong.

"Shifters can be as clique-ish as vampires," Cassie explains as we make our way outside for our first group project. "Wolves stick to wolves, panthers stick to panthers, merfolk stick to..."

"Merfolk. Yeah, I get it. Everyone here is a bigot."

The vamps are all huddled in a group, laughing and talking in the sunshine. Cassie told me they wear a special spray-on sunscreen. SPF 200. That must be why it always takes Tina so long in the bathroom every morning.

Our instructor is a fit woman called Artemis—yes, *that* Artemis, the goddess of wild animals and hunting. I'm finally starting to know these things without having to ask Cassie thanks to a "Dummies Guide to Greek Mythology" book I found in the library. Artemis explains that each assassin has to pair up with a tracker, the goal being to see how well we work together. I'm immediately nervous. No tracker is going to want to pair with me, since I'm a super novice assassin.

But one of the shifters approaches me with a smile.

So far, with the exception of Cassie, everyone else at school has been a little standoffish. Or actually a lot. During every meal Cassie and I sit alone at our giant empty table in the dining room. It probably doesn't help that I still haven't been able to release my inner whatever. Not that I've been trying too hard. Keeping up with classes has keeps me so busy that I don't have time for much else. And, there's also the fact that I'm maybe still a little scared of finding out exactly what those glowing eyes belong to. Still, I can't forget Themis's warning—the clock is ticking.

But I don't exactly want the tracker who has picked me. He's a bat. Also, a bit batty. He's always staring at me!

"Greg," I say, trying to force a smile.

"Edie." His grin twitches as he approaches me. "I've been thinking. We should mate."

I blink. "Whaaat?"

"You know, have sex."

"I know what it means. Why would I..."

"Well, there aren't that many of us bat shifters left, so we should probably procreate soon."

A few vampires overhear us and start chanting, "mate, mate, mate." I glare at them and they immediately fall silent. That's been happening ever since I set Val on fire. Which... I turn, and glare at Greg.

"You do know I breathe fire when I get excited?"

He nods. "Yeah, and I'll admit that was worrying. But then I realized. We'll just do it batty style." Greg mimes like he's...what is he doing? Pretending to direct traffic while thrusting his hips and—

Ooooh. I got it now.

"We are not having sex batty style or any other way!" I shake my head. "Absolutely not. No dates. No shacking up. No—"

Greg cuts me off. "Oh, no. Don't get me wrong. I don't want to date you or anything."

"You just want me to birth your bat babies?"

"Exactly," he says. I try to back away but Artemis appears next to us.

"Great, you guys are a pair."

"Oh no," I look around but there's no one left. I'm stuck with bat boy.

"Greg, your job is to locate the minotaur's lair, taking Edie with you to complete the assassination." She stops, turns to me, her mouth a thin line.

"You understand that you are not to actually kill anyone, correct? No more fires?"

I nod. Smart-assing Artemis is not cool. She pinned a kid to the wall last week for it. Like, actually, with arrows.

"You have forty minutes. This is a pass/fail test." She looks at me. "We'll see how well you do and determine if you need extra tutoring. I'm thinking you do."

My stomach tightens nervously with my typical test anxiety. I push it away and turn to Greg. "So let's..." but Greg is gone. In his place flaps a bat, making awkward zig zagging patterns in the air. A tiny little uniform—complete with wee plaid tie—covers his little bat body.

I close my eyes. Please, don't let me be a bat.

"Follow me," he squeaks and flies off. I run after him, hoping that I can keep up.

"Did you just talk to me...in *bat*?" I huff as I catch up to him.

"Yup," he nods his little bat head as he squeaks yet again. A noise which my brain is somehow able to translate into words. Crazy. "All shifters can understand each other when in animal form. Witches can usually understand a few words here or there. Vampires, though, are big fat zeroes when it comes to animal linguistics. You can shift and talk shit right to their face and they don't have a clue!"

Greg squeak laughs at this and I can't help but join in.

Remembering that we're in the middle of an assignment, we focus back on our task. We're supposed to be tracking a fellow classmate, someone Artemis pulled out of first period and sent off into the woods. Greg swoops and swerves a few feet ahead of me, and I'm following dutifully when something occurs to me.

"Hey, aren't bats blind?"

Greg stops mid-air, then comes to perch on my shoulder. His wing brushes my cheek and I try not to shrink away from him.

"Eh...not exactly blind, no. But I can't see very well."

"And you're a tracker?"

"I'm a *bad* tracker," he says, squeaky voice going even higher. "But what I can do is smell."

"Great," I mutter.

"It is great, know why? Because werewolves are awesome trackers...and they stink."

It's almost funny. I kind of smile, but quickly wipe it off my face in case he offers to impregnate me again.

"And huge," he adds, pointing to a spot in the under-brush that has been completely flattened.

"Oh, okay," I say, walking through it, Greg still on my shoulder. "So we just follow the path of destruction?"

"Pretty much."

We're the last to make it to the meet up point, but we're under the time limit. I'm proud of myself–I didn't freeze up even with a tiny little bat riding on my shoulder. His little bat claws are clinging to my hair; I brush him off and he flutters away, turning back into a boy.

He grins. "We make a great team. We should definitely have children together."

"Okay, is this weird preoccupation with procreation a *you* thing, or a *shifter* thing?"

He shrugs his shoulders. "Not all shifters have to worry about the continued existence of their race. The winged ones, we're a little more rare. Bats, harpies, owls, ostriches."

"Ostriches," I say, waiting for him to crack a smile, or let me know he's joking. He doesn't.

Please, I think. *Please don't make me a bat or an ostrich.*

"Have you molted yet?" Greg asks, and I decide I'm done with him. I back away while he's still talking. "Wait...we should set up a time to..."

I don't let him finish. I turn and basically run to go find Cassie instead.

"How'd it go?" I ask when I find her.

"Fine. My shifter ditched me so I just saw where to go."

"You followed the werewolves too?" I ask.

"No, I mean like"—she rolls her eyes back into her head —"*saw*. Except first my sight took me to the bathroom, because apparently I'm going to develop a urinary tract infection."

"That's terrible," I say. "But at least your shifter abandoned you rather than suggested you two have bat sex."

Cassie laughs. "Yeah, that's Greg for you. He's really into

being a bat. If there's even a chance that you're one too, he's not going to leave you alone."

"Hey, Edie." Suddenly Val is at my side. He's so quiet, I didn't even hear him approach. Vampires definitely have an unfair advantage. "Look, if you're not busy with Greg—"

"I will *never* be busy with Greg."

This actually earns a full smile. A fleeting one, but I catch it just the same. "Anyway, I just wanted to let you know there's a full moon party tonight."

"Oh?" I ask, trying to sound cool and hoping that he can't tell my heart is beating madly. Is Val asking me to this party?

"Yeah, it's mostly a shifter thing, but vamps and parties. You know."

I have no idea at all, but I nod like I understand. "Totally."

"Right." He nods back. "So I just wanted to ask..." He hesitates and I wonder if beneath the super cool guy exterior, he might actually be a little bit bashful. His eyes meet mine. They are dark and intense, stealing my breath as he asks, "Can you keep an eye on Tina? She goes a little overboard at these things sometimes. If she gets out of hand, I'd appreciate if you'd come get me."

My heart sinks so slowly, I can almost trace its journey. "Sure," I manage to say at last. "of course I'll keep an eye on her." Somehow I fake a laugh. "Vampires and parties, right? What can ya do?"

Val's mouth curls in that slightly mocking way that seems to suggest he sees right through me. He holds out a piece of paper. "My room number. In case you need me."

Our fingers brush as I take the paper. And then finally, Val walks away.

"Wow," Cassie shakes her head. "For a minute there I

was worried he was getting ready to ask you to the party. That would've been terrible."

"Yeah," I agree. "Cause vampires get totally wild and crazy at parties, right?"

Cassie gives me one of those looks that means I've got it totally backwards. I've gotten to know that look too well over the past few weeks. "No. They like to just stand around looking above it all and making fun of everyone else."

"Sooo, what do you think Val meant about Tina getting out of hand?" I ask nervously.

"Oh, he's definitely worried she's gonna bite you," Cassie replies.

"Great. So nice of Val to warn me."

"Actually, it kinda was." Cassie gives me a searching look. "Do you think he might sorta like you?"

I roll my eyes. "Definitely not. And I for sure do not like him," I lie, hoping it will help make it true. "He's just a guy I once set on fire."

Cassie doesn't look totally convinced. "Okay, well, that's good. It's better to stay away from that one," she tells me. "He's got a reputation."

"What, as a heartbreaker?" I ask, watching him walk away in his floaty way. That is actually the saying on the sparkly purple t-shirt he's wearing today. It still blows my mind that Tina makes them. Usually the only creativity she shows is in finding new ways to insult me and make my life miserable.

"Um, tear your eyes away from his torso, Edie. That guy is more than just a heartbreaker. It's more like he'll rip your heart out of your chest and dance on it. Seriously. There's a second year who quit because he broke up with her."

I shake my head. "I'm not going to let some guy make me

quit. I need this place." I'm almost surprised by how true this has become. It's not that I'm happy here. There's too much that's new and weird and stressful and just plain difficult for me to even imagine enjoying myself. But unlike when I was living with the foster people, I have a purpose here.

And also, okay, there are a lot of hot guys. I'm not gonna pretend that isn't a perk or that it doesn't brighten my days, because it does.

She nods. "Okay, well, let's get lunch and I'll walk you to remedial flying."

As we head to the dining hall I can't help but search for Val in the crowd. With that purple shirt he should be easy to find. Also, I've noticed over the past few weeks that while he's always with the vampires, he tends to stand slightly apart from them.

"Looking for anyone in particular?" Cassie asks in an arch tone.

"Um, no, I was just wondering..." I search my brain for something I might've been thinking, but I'm saved by Cassie's eyes rolling back in her head.

She throws her arms out and falls to the ground proclaiming in an eerily loud voice, "The tuna will be bad. The tuna, the tuna. Beware the fish, for it will make you—"

"Hey!" I actually interrupt her vision by shaking her, even though the damage is already done.

"Wait, I wanted to hear more about the bad tuna," Tina mocks. "Sounds like a campus-wide food poisoning issue. Which end will it come out of? It's such a mystery!"

Cassie only shakes in my arms. I wish she'd stand up for herself—like, actually, but also literally. She's getting heavy.

Tina's friend Jenn hops up and does an impromptu reenactment of Cassie's vision, throwing herself on the ground and writhing, gripping her stomach. Too bad there's no drama club here; she's really good. If only it wasn't at Cassie's expense.

She's finally standing on her own, but she's got her face covered, like she can't stand to watch Jenn's antics.

"Jenn, you are hilarious," Tina laughs.

"Yeah, sounds like a good time at dinner tonight," Marguerite, another of Tina's cronies, adds and they laugh. "Real shits and giggles."

"Just ignore them," I tell Cassie.

Her face is beet red. But Tina won't give it a rest. She marches over and gets in Cassie's face. "You know, if your prophecies actually mattered maybe you wouldn't be bounced around from one discipline to another. Everyone knows you're only here because of your mom."

"Whoa," I say. "Back off."

Tina flashes her fangs at me, a strand of green hair slipping out from behind her ear. "And you...why are *you* here at all? Swamper."

One of the teachers walks over to us, all imposing and god-like, and to my relief Tina actually backs off. She rejoins her crew but before she sits she takes her tie and makes a hanging motion. The meaning is clear. I'm on her shit list. Well, not really a surprise.

Cassie looks mortified, so I try desperately to change the subject.

"So what's the deal with the vamps not wearing their uniforms to regulation, anyway?"

"What? Oh that." Cassie shrugs. "You know vamps."

"I'm starting to." *And one in particular who I'd like to know more...* I quickly shut down that train of thought.

I've got her on a new thought track though and she rolls with it. "I mean, they're sorta anarchists at heart. And deeply, deeply selfish. Which is why dating one would be a bad idea."

"Well yeah. Obviously." I force a fake laugh. We get our lunch and walk to an empty table in the corner. No need to call more attention to ourselves.

She's full steam ahead now. "My mom actually remembers when they were first debating about letting them into the Academy. Shifters and witches were here from the beginning, and vampires always seemed like a perfect fit. I mean everyone knows vampires love to kill. They're natural assassins and they have no conscience or respect for life."

"I don't really see the problem there," I can't help observing.

"Right. You'd think so. Except vamps have this weird thing where they'll get super attached to someone and it's like no matter what happens after that,they're loyal to the very end."

"Again, that seems not so bad." I say, playing with my food.

"No, it's awful. The gods want us to be loyal to them first. Above friends, family, and even ourselves. But a vampire... well, like Val, for instance. He was super attached to his old roommate. They were best friends. And the roommate wasn't even a vampire. He was a werewolf. But then—" Cassie suddenly stops talking.

Flustered, she laughs. "Why am I talking about this? You asked me about uniforms. So anyway, the vamps don't shift so they add other, non-magic apparel stuff. The shifters are essentially practical and pragmatic creatures, so they appreciate that the uniforms are made to magically shift with them. And the magic types are unbending rule followers. They think the world will dissolve into chaos if they don't do everything by the book. And if it's a book of magic we're talking about—well, that could be true.

"Oh, and Tina's hair. I mean, they could have just let her in for her hair, am I right? I mean, like wow. Her punk look is totally awesome, jives with her whole *I might kill you* thing."

Cassie is so very obviously trying to change the subject, but it's a good time for me to ask something I've been curious about.

"Seriously," I agree. "I wish I could get highlights like that."

"Isn't that a thing in the real world?" Cassie asks, clearly confused. "They're called salons, right?"

"No, I mean, I wish I could get them like she does." I pick up a piece of my hair and pinch it, pulling downwards like I saw Tina do, turning her tresses green. "Pretty cool, right? She just like wills her hair to be the color she wants."

"Um, no," Cassie shakes her head emphatically. "That would be a shifter trick, and there's no way Tina's got some shifter in her. Nobody is more proud of being pure vampire than that girl."

"But..." I'm going to argue, but decide not to. I thought I saw Tina tweaking her hair, but that was my first day here. I was a mess, and I also thought her Venus fly trap was breathing so it's possible I'd just had a really long day.

I open my mouth to go back to the whole Val and his roommate story, certain I can get Cassie to spill everything. But before I can, she looks down at her wrist. There's no watch there, but that doesn't stop her from saying, "Oh wow, look at the time. I gotta go be somewhere else that isn't here with you. So, okay, catch ya later. Bye!"

And with that she runs off, leaving me alone at the table.

I watch her go, stunned that for the first time Cassie has had enough of me before I've had enough of her.

13

Remedial flying is taught by a crusty harpy named Ocypete with no people skills.

Actually, she has amazing people skills. Berating people skills. I'm the only one in the class, and weeks into my lessons with her, she's highly frustrated with me. Although I did finally figure out how to say her name, I whisper it to myself on the walk to class every day, just in case. "Ms. Ah-sip-pity."

I got it right on the first try today, but she's still irritated with me.

"Do I look like a Ms. to you?" she spits.

"Sorry, it's just a habit from my old school—"

"Yes, you've brought a lot of habits from your old school. You were a mediocre student there too, weren't you?"

That hurts. "I was a bad test taker."

"Pfffft." I've never had a teacher give me raspberries before. It's shockingly effective because I'm immediately ashamed of myself.

"Tests have nothing to do with it," Ocypete says. "You're afraid and you're holding back."

I think of the eyes inside me, the red ones I see sometimes when I close my own. Ocypete's not wrong. They do scare me. But I don't appreciate having it pointed out, and I definite don't like it when she pokes a claw into my soft belly.

"It's time to let all of you out," she says.

"I don't know how to shift. Nobody's teaching me! And Themis said there was a spell holding me back from—"

"Themis doesn't know her ass from her elbow. And no one is taught how to shift. You just do it. In fact, it's a lot like flying. You're the only thing around here with wings that can't fly," she rants at me, popping a pair of dusty-winged feathers out of her back. She rises a few feet in the air, but it's not a lesson, she's just that irritated with me. I immediately feel awful.

"I'm sorry," I say, for about the fiftieth time since our lessons together began. My wings—a faded dull rose now—droop at my sides. "I didn't even know I *had* wings until, like, a few weeks ago."

She puts her own away. "I heard you've kept them in all this time. That must have been painful."

"Yes," I tell her, hoping for some sympathy. Instead she's suddenly got hold of my ear and I'm on the ground, her bony fingers digging into the side of my skull. It hurts like hell because she doesn't exactly have fingers. More like claws. Nasty, curled, withered little bird claws.

"Well it's going to hurt a lot more if a monster gets a hold of you and you can't get your ass off the ground."

"Wow, okay, okay." I hold up my hands in surrender even though I'm already face planting. I couldn't be more surrendered, unless I roll over and show her my belly. She lets go of my ear and I get to my feet. Something runs down the side of my neck.

I swipe at it, and my fingers come away bloody.

"Hey!" I say. "Are you really allowed to just hurt me?" It's a question I've asked more than once, since her hurting me has become a thing. She's never actually answered me.

She doesn't show any sympathy even at the sight of my blood, which she's never managed to spill before. Instead she hops—literally hops—forward and licks my hand. I jump back, pulling my fingers with me in case she decides to go for more.

"Gross," I say.

"Hmm..." She rolls her tongue in her mouth, tasting my blood. "Not a harpy, like me...not a bat either."

"I'm not an ostrich, am I?" I ask.

She thinks about it for a second, shakes her head, then spits. "No, but I can't really say for sure what you are. Let's see those wings again," she says, noticing that I'd tucked them away.

I comply, a little embarrassed that they're gray now. A defeated, unhappy gray. She circles me.

"Scaled, not feathered," she says to herself. "Interesting. Regardless, it doesn't matter what you are if you don't know how to use them. Pay attention."

"I have been paying attention!"

And it's true. I've listened attentively as she lectured me on running starts, triple wing pumps, and adjusting your arms and legs to cut down on wind shear.

When I can't even get off the ground again today, she decides to focus on posture instead, instructing me on how to keep my arms and legs as close to my body as possible, even when I'm just standing around.

"If you really want to eliminate wind shear, you should cut your breasts off," she informs me, to which I politely decline.

"Suit yourself," she says, showing me her own, trim silhouette. "I can rise a hundred feet in a second."

"And I can get laid," I tell her, which she actually laughs at.

By the end of the hour I'm covered in grass stains from wiping out so many times, my hair is a windblown mess, and I've got more bumps and bruises then I usually do when I leave Kratos' class. But my wings are a bright jade green, and there's a bounce in my step when I ask Ocypete if I can start calling her Pity for short.

"It'll be ironic," I tell her.

"Fine, if I can call you *talented*," she says.

"I said ironic, not sarcastic," I mumble. Ocypete actually laughs at that.

Maybe I'm growing on her.

"Well, you're the worst flyer I've ever seen." She tells me. "No sarcasm there."

I sigh. Maybe not.

Luckily, Tina isn't in our room when I get back and Cassie is still avoiding me. But instead of laying down, I dig under my mattress for Dad's phone. I've had it with me ever since I picked it up from the ruins of the greenhouse where he died. I thought there might be something on it to help me figure out what was going on, or at the very least, see his texts and calls. Dad obviously knew something I didn't, and maybe he was talking about it with other people.

But it hadn't mattered. I'd been elated back in foster care just to see it power on—confident answers were taps away. Instead, I'd been faced with a lock screen with the old pass-code—0309—not working. Dad must have changed it.

He must've been in a hurry, though—or too technologically challenged—to put a limit on passcode attempts. I've got all the tries I need to crack this thing. I've tried combinations of birthdays, holidays, anniversaries, with no luck. So I got methodical and started with 0001, and then 0002, and so forth. I've been at this for six months, and tonight I'm diving in with 0589.

I know there are about a million options. I'm sure there's some sort of formula I could use to find out the depressing amount of actual number combination possibilities, but Hermes wasn't lying about one thing—there's no signal at Mount Olympus. I can't use my phone, but I can keep it charged and access anything saved on it. So the same will be true of Dad's, if I can get it open.

I'm tapping in 0600 when it occurs to me that I'm at a school with people who turn into bats, suck people's blood —and accurately predict what's going to be for breakfast. Why am I sitting here guessing when I can just ask Cassie for help?

Cassie also rooms with a vampire, but apparently she prefers to share a coffin with her boyfriend at night, so Cassie essentially has the room to herself. Cassie has begged me to ask for a transfer, but while Tina may be a bitch, at least she's quiet sometimes.

I knock on the door. Cassie opens it a crack and peers out. For a second I'm worried she'll slam it in my face, but then she flings it open all the way. The next thing I know, she's dragged me into room and is sprawled across her bed in a dramatic pose.

"Fine. I'll talk. I can't take the torture of being apart anymore."

I blink. And then slowly sit on her roommate's bare mattress. "Um, okay."

Cassie looks at me intently. "Swear you will tell no one

what I've told you. Or that I've told you. No one is supposed to speak of this. Ever."

I hesitate. "What are we talking about?"

"Fine, you've twisted my arm. I will tell you the story of Val and his werewolf roommate."

"Okaaay. Let's have it, then."

Cassie sits cross-legged on her bed and folds her hands in her lap. "It all began when the new shifter started here a year ago. Emmie was a cat shifter. And, well, she was also my roommate. Everyone loved her. Val's roommate, Derrick, he really loved her, like looooveeed–"

I hold up my hand to stop her. I get it. Cassie shrugs.

"She was just one of those people. You know?"

I do know. Mavis was like that. *Is* like that.

Sometimes it annoyed me, which seems so petty now. It just felt like everything was always just so easy for her. Friends. Romance. School. Anything she wanted fell into her lap.

Now, though...now I'd give anything to see her again. To have one of our movie nights where we'd spend an hour arguing over what we'd watch before finally deciding to just pig out on pizza while some makeover show played in the background.

I miss her so much it hurts.

"Anyway," Cassie continues, "Emmie left school after a few months and they said it was a leave of absence, but apparently she was on some super-secret mission with another student. Exciting, right? It's amazing Emmie was sent, being so new, but she was the most naturally talented tracker the school had ever seen. But then, the worst thing happened—they were captured by the monsters. The other student died, but Emmie got away. When she returned to the Academy—"

"Wait." I spring up from the bed. "I know this story. Ms. Themis told me. The girl became a traitor and then fled. And her boyfriend—who must have been Val's roommate—went with her."

Cassie's mouth hangs open. She is totally and completely deflated. "Why didn't you tell me you already knew?"

"I didn't know that I knew."

"Hmm…" Cassie considers this for a moment and seems to accept it. "Well, yeah. They escaped. There was like a terrible awful storm that night. I'm talking downpour, and that might have helped Emmie escape. That's the flip side of being an amazing tracker—you also know how to cover your own."

I shrug. "Sorry. And…I actually came to talk with you about something else entirely."

Cassie perks up. "Oh?"

I pull Dad's phone from my pocket.

Cassie's eyes become huge. "Oh my gods! Is that a cell phone! I've heard of those! Let's order pizza from Pizza House. And then prank call people and ask if their car is running!"

"Cassie…" I hesitate, trying to find a good way to put this. "You may want to consider getting off campus and seeing a bit of the real world. I think it might help you understand it better."

"Oh wow, I'd love to do that." Her eyes glow. "Let's go together this summer! You can show me all the sights!"

I sigh. I was actually planning on hiding out at the Academy as long as possible. Here I can forget about all I lost, but outside of the gates there would be a million painful reminders.

"Listen," I say, switching the subject without making any

promises. "I haven't really told you much about my family and where I come from..."

"Understatement of the year."

She's right. I haven't told Cassie anything. And it's not like she hasn't asked. Despite liking to talk, she isn't the type to monopolize every conversation. She's also deeply curious about life "on the outside" and is constantly pumping me for information about the non-Academy world. Maybe I have some trust issues after my friendships imploded last year. It's also hard to talk about everything that happened and have to relive it all again.

Which is why I plan to give Cassie the bare minimum details. Somehow, though, once I start talking it all spills out of me.

Finally, I finish with, "I thought I knew my dad. But he was hiding secrets about me from me. And who knows what else. I need answers. I need—" I need my dad back. But I don't say that aloud. Instead, I hold the phone out to Cassie. "Could you do your eyes rolling back into your head thing and try to see the code?"

Cassie takes the phone and looks down at it. After a moment she makes a low humming noise in her throat. I sit forward eagerly.

She looks back up at me. "Sorry, I'm getting nothing. It's hard to read tech without having a connection to the person it belongs to."

"Oh." I slump, more disappointed than I have any right to be.

"But," Cassie adds. "We could try getting our hands on a Seer Stone."

"Seer Stone?"

"Yeah, they have a few in the vault. They're sacred so they're kept with the other important artifacts. My mom...

well, my mom would never break the rules but I know my way around down there. If we see anyone, though, you might have to distract them until I can find a Seer Stone and well, touch it—it will enhance my power. But it's a risk. If we get caught, we'll be in trouble for sure."

I nod, not quite understanding. "So the stones are worth this risk because…?"

"If I get my grabby hands on one of these stones *and* I'm also holding your dad's phone, presto! Login code seen!"

I spring to my feet. "What are we waiting for? Let's go."

14

Cassie leads me out of the dorms and around the back of the school. From the center of campus comes the typical sounds of a party. Music. Voices raised in laughter. And wolves howling. Okay, not *all* the typical sounds.

"I forgot about the party," I say, looking up where sure enough a full moon is overhead.

I also forgot about my promise to watch Tina. Or watch her fangs so they don't accidentally sink into my neck. It's probably best I'm not anywhere near her right now. Too late, it occurs to me that Callie might've wanted to attend the party.

"You weren't planning on going, were you?"

"Nah, it's not my scene." Cassie shrugs. "When Emmie was here we'd go together and it was fun, but now that she's gone everyone just ignores me or makes fun of me."

"Yeah, I get it. I've had some bad party experiences too. People suck." Cassie nods in agreement and yet I can't help but look back toward the party sounds and wonder what a certain guy who definitely sucks is up to right now.

"This way," Cassie says, taking a turn that leads us

back into the swamp. There's some Greek-looking ruins, crumbling pillars and statues.

"Um, I know we're in the assassination class but you're not taking me out here to kill me for extra credit or anything, are you?"

Cassie throws me a wounded look. "I would never! We're besties!" She motions toward the ruins of a building, stone steps descending into the earth. "This is just the secret way to get to the vault. Come on!" She jogs down the steps and I can't do anything but follow.

The corridor is damp and dirty. Creeping vines hang along the stone walls and as I peer closer several giant spiders quickly scurry away. As I quickly jump back, Cassie fiddles with something in her pocket, and a light goes on.

"It's super dark down here. I'm glad I remembered my flashlight."

We walk along the corridor until it slopes up slightly, leaving the spiders and brackish puddles behind. Cassie motions to an ancient-looking door, slightly ajar. On the other side is a normal, if dusty, room. It's filled with artifacts, from pottery to gold coins to stone busts and jewelry.

"This is the non-magical objects room," Cassie explains. "No one ever comes in here. It's just junk."

Sure, ancient priceless artifacts are junk. I don't argue. She leads us to the other side of the room and turns off her flashlight. "Let's peek around the corner," she whispers. "See if the way is clear."

I open the door a bit and have a peek. The way is definitely not clear.

Standing just a few feet away is Hermes. He's speaking to an older gentleman who is wearing a toga. Obviously the toga thing goes with the whole ancient Greek vibe here, but it's still hard not to think of it as a silly costume.

The older dude moves a bit and his outfit choice becomes more obvious. The man knows how to rock a toga. Which is to say: he's ripped. With all the six-packs walking around this school you'd think I was attending Mount Olympus Gym Rat Academy. The sight of rippling abs has almost become humdrum. But the toga guy has the type of abs that Men's Health double-page spreads are made of. His six-pack is more like an eight-pack and his arms are sculpted like a Greek god.

"That's Mr. Zee!" Cassie squeaks in my ear and I shoot her a look. I hold my breath, hoping they didn't hear her, but Hermes continues.

"I just don't understand the need for secrecy," Hermes is saying. "Bats don't spontaneously set themselves on fire. An accident of this magnitude—"

"We don't know it was an accident. I will not sow the seeds of fear and dissent." Toga guy—er, Mr. Zee—has one of those super deep commanding voices. I bet even when he says, "I gotta take a piss," it comes out like he's ordering an army to advance and kill.

Hermes raises his voice. "Well, if it wasn't an accident, that's an even better reason to inform the students. They need to protect themselves."

Mr. Zee puts a hand on Hermes' shoulder. "We will protect them. We always have." He pulls Hermes in closer. "Now, let's retire—"

Hermes shakes his head. "You're not going to distract me with sex. Well, maybe you will. You're lucky you're so hot."

My eyes widen as they share a wet slurping kiss. After several long moments they part, both panting hard.

"Let's find someplace more comfortable," Mr. Zee says. Hermes quickly answers in the affirmative and the two walk down the hall and disappear.

"Did you hear that?" I ask Cassie.

"What, Hermes and Mr. Zee? Yeah, everyone knows they bang. Hermes is the most sexually fluid person in the world. He even tried to come on to Ocypete at one point—she almost gouged his eyes out as a rejection!"

Hmm. Well, there goes my feeling special about having a god flirt with me. Apparently Hermes will make a move on anything. With a shake of my head, I refocus on the more important thing here.

"No, they said there was an accident! What if we're in danger?"

She pauses. "Do you want to go back?"

"No." We've come too far. "Where are the Seer Stones?"

"Across the hall. If it's clear, I'll lead the way."

I double check that no one else is lurking in the halls. "Yeah, it's clear."

Cassie leads me to another room, but this one is better kept. It's full of books and objects, which Cassie informs me are all magical. Some glow from within, but most just look ordinary. Like, how is a frying pan magical? Does it make perfect frittatas?

"Here!" Cassie calls from across the room where she's opening drawers in a cabinet. I rush to her side. There's a stone the size of a Venti Starbucks cup. It's gray and kind of boring looking, really.

"That's it?" I ask.

Cassie nods, her eyes wide. "My mom always warned me against touching them. I think she's afraid ramping up my abilities will be too much for me."

"Wait, it won't be harmful, will it?"

"No, Probably not. Maybe," she says uncertainly.

"If you don't feel comfortable," I tell her, my heart sinking.

"This is for a good cause," she quickly replies, now determined. She holds out her hand. "Give me your dad's phone."

I do and she places her other hand on the stone. It flashes a brilliant white light and Cassie's eyes roll back in her head.

"9372." Smoke pours from the stone, and flows around her. "The answers you seek will lead to ruin. The father you want is not the father you had. Beware, the light is coming for you."

What does it all mean? That bit about my father sends a chill through my whole body. A second later Cassie releases the stone and blinks at me. "Wow. That's a rush. I..." She's blushing a little bit. "Sorry if that upset you. The bit about beware the light and all. Sounded pretty dangerous, huh?"

I swallow. "Yeah."

"Well, I wouldn't worry about it too much. You know me and my prophecies. It probably just means that you're going to get a bad sunburn or something."

She looks at my dad's phone, still unlocked in my hand.

"And it's okay if you don't want to get into your dad's phone. Sure we risked a lot to get down here and were almost caught by Mr. Zee himself. Also, using the Seer Stone is kinda giving me heartburn, but it's fine if—"

"Okay! I'll do it. Just, please...be quiet for a minute."

Cassie opens her mouth to say something, but then quickly closes it again.

I take a deep breath. The truth is, no matter how bad whatever I find might be, it's better than not knowing. I type the digits into the phone.

"We're in!" I tell her as I look at Dad's home screen.

Now that I have access, I don't even know where to start. I try his email, but it's just a bunch of boring old sales notices and stuff from work. Then I notice he has some voicemails. They must have all downloaded before I came to the Academy, because there's no WiFi here. Several are junk calls, but I freeze when I come to the date of the rogue wave.

It's from Layla. Aka Mom.

The time stamp is from the exact moment Dad and I were running up the stairs, escaping from the waters. It doesn't look like Dad ever listened to it.

My hand trembles as I press play.

"Danny, they're here. I think they may have gotten to Mavis too. Get Edie to the safe house. I'll try to hold them off as long as I can." Her voice is strained and hurried. And yet also so very much Mom. Tears stream down my face.

"What is going on in here, ladies?" I hear from behind me, while at the same time on the voicemail, there's a loud crash and then Mom says, "I love you. Tell Edie I love her and Mavis too, if she's..." A sob. "Just tell them both—"

That's it. The message ends. I stand frozen, while Cassie gasps, "Themis!"

Slowly, I turn to face Themis. "This is a restricted area. You could both be expelled for this."

Cassie, bless her heart, tries to deflect. "I wanted to show Edie the Seer Stones and what I can really do. I was trying to impress her!"

"No!" I can't let her take the fall. "I'm responsible. I insisted."

Themis evaluates us and her eyes immediately go to Dad's cell phone in my hand. "You're not supposed to have that." She holds out a hand. "Please give it to me now."

I clutch the phone to my chest. "No. I wasn't calling anyone. Hermes said there was no point in bringing it, but he didn't say I couldn't have it."

"You are mistaken. You are also in a restricted area. The

ice on which you are skating is very thin." Themis
stretches her hand out further. "Ms. Evans, I will not ask
twice."

I gulp and consider running for it, when without my
control, my arm stretches out and my fingers release the
phone, dropping it into Themis' waiting hand.

"What!" I gasp. "You can't control me! That's gotta be
against the rules."

"I would never do anything against the rules!" She
snaps. "What I do is anything that's needed to enforce them.
If you do not like it we can begin the Academy removal
procedures tomorrow."

Cassie grabs hold of my arm with two hands. "Edie," she
whispers. "Leave it."

Rage. Despair. And the ache of hearing my mother's
voice after all this time, churn inside me. Somehow I force
myself to say, "Yes, ma'am. I mean, no, ma'am. I do not want
to be removed from the Academy."

"That's what I thought." She nods and slips the phone
into a pocket in her skirt. "It's late. I think you ladies ought
to get into bed now. I will escort you to the dorm."

And she does, like we're children caught sneaking a late
night snack. There's nothing else to say as we're marched up
through the archive room and to our dorm building. Cassie
and I both shuffle along. I notice that all the party noises are
gone and wonder if Themis broke that up too. It is only once
we're inside front door of our dorms that Cassie says, "That
was weird."

"The Jedi mind trick, you mean?"

"I don't know what that means. But what I meant was
Themis didn't send us to Mr. Zee. She just let us leave."

I close my eyes and bite back sobs. I haven't felt this low
since the day I first arrived at the foster people's house.

"What does it matter? Dad's phone and any answers it held are gone."

"Well..." Cassie hesitates. "Not quite."

"You think we can steal it back from Themis?"

A high whinnying laugh comes out of Cassie. "Noooo. Are you suicidal? Steal from Themis. That's—no." She continues to chuckle nervously. "I was thinking more like, that phone might've had answers, but there are answers in other places too. Like maybe in the archives. Where my mother works. Whatever your dad's connection to the Academy was—someone will have recorded it and filed it away at some point. We just have to find it."

I spin toward Cassie and grab both of her hands. A new urgency is inside of me. After getting so close to answers and having that little taste of mom's voice, I need more. "When can we go? Tonight? Tomorrow?"

Her eyes go wide. "Tonight might be pushing our luck. We wouldn't want to bump into Themis again. But tomorrow night...I think we could do it then."

"Tomorrow," I agree. "We get answers tomorrow."

15

The mood in the cafeteria the next day is weird. I mean, weirder than normal. Which is pretty freaking strange.

The vamps are all talking snidely behind their hands and making faces over at a table of shifters—Greg and his friends. I spot Fern the medic at another table with her witch friends. I wave and she waves back.

"What's going on?" I asked Cassie as I slide into the seat across from her. She always knows the latest gossip.

Her eyes go wide. "Haven't you heard?! Apparently one of the bat boys got kicked out of school because he kept shifting and flying in front of the girls' assassination class dormitory bathroom windows. The vamps are seriously pissed."

"A bat? Really? Who saw this? Who saw him leave?"

Cassie shrugs. "I don't know. That's not really the interesting part of the story."

"Cassie." I lean forward and lower my voice to make sure no one else overhears. "Last night, we heard Hermes mention a bat boy having an accident that involved him being set on fire. They wanted to keep it a secret. Don't you think pretending he got kicked out would be a good way to do that?"

"Oh no," she shakes her head. "They would never do that."

I pause, trying to remember exactly what we heard. "I don't know." But if someone was injured maybe Fern knows.

"Right. So I'm sure it's fine." Cassie smiles brightly and I can tell this is a topic she doesn't want to discuss. Which is not something that happens often. I drop it for now.

"Okay, then, let's talk about tonight. How much sneaking is required for us to get into the archives?"

"Who's sneaking?" Greg asks, thumping his lunch tray beside me. He lowers himself onto the bench, sitting close enough that his thigh presses tightly against my own.

I dig my elbow in his ribs. "We've got a whole table here. You don't have to sit on top of me." I don't really want him here, but then I remember that the rest of the school is currently ignoring him too, by direction of the vamps, so I ease up, removing my elbow.

Greg shifts away from me, but not far. "You can sit here," I tell him. "But I'm not granting you access to my vagina."

Greg makes a face. "Do you have to use the v-word? It's kinda..." Noticing the look on my face, he has enough brains in his head not to continue along that road of thought. "I mean, yeah, I do want your...vagina..." He nearly chokes on the word. "But I've decided it's more than that. I also want your heart now, too." He grins at me like a puppy that has successfully performed a trick and now expects a treat.

I shake my head. "Greg, I feel like someone has been giving you purposely terrible advice."

"No way!" Judging by the way he clutches his heart, I've mortally offended him. "My bros got my back." Greg gestures to the table two down from ours, where the rest of the pariahs are sitting. They are watching us with undisguised interest.

Cassie grins and waves enthusiastically. "Oh hi!" She pauses and then adds in a slightly higher, strained voice, "Hi Darcy!"

Oh boy. Cassie has a crush on one of those little goonies.

I think about how she helped me out last night. And how she's gonna do it again tonight—at much greater risk to herself and her mother—even though she hasn't mentioned either of those things once. Plus, those guys don't have a chance with the vamps giving them the stink eye.

It's horribly awfully depressingly clear what I need to do.

"Greg, there's lots of room here. Why don't your friends join us?"

Greg looks from me to his friends and then back to me. "Oh, I don't know. They'll cramp my style."

"Go get them, Greg. Now."

Greg goes.

"Oh my!" Cassie squeals, her hands fluttering around her face like two butterflies in their final death throes. "Do you think they'll come over? Oh look, they're getting up. All of them. Even Darcy."

"And he's special why?" I ask, fully expecting Cassie to spill everything at the slightest prompting. But apparently there are some cards even she holds close to her chest. Even if the poor girl doesn't realize they're backwards so everyone can see them.

"Oh no," she says. "He's just a merman shifter. He stays during summer holidays and we've bumped into each other at the lagoon a few times. It's where the merfolk hang out."

Her face goes bright red and I wonder exactly how much bumping went on at the lagoon.

After lots of rearranging and scooching we're all seated together at the now snug table. Greg is unfortunately beside me once more. And Cassie...well, she looks like she could die happy.

I expect this to be the longest most painful meal of my life, but amazingly end up enjoying myself. The guys are dweebs extraordinaire, but it's actually refreshing after all the ultra-handsome alpha dudes that seem to make up most of the male population here. Just when I decide that it might be nice to make this a regular thing, Greg turns to me and, pulling a crushed flower from his pocket, holds it out to me.

"Edie, would you consider being my date for Persephone's Spring Fling?"

"No," I say immediately. His face falls like I kicked his puppy. Guilt tugs at me. I hate to crush him in front of all his friends. "I mean, I don't even know what that is."

Cassie rushes to fill me in. "It's a dance. Persephone returns to the campus every year in the spring. She's the goddess of the underworld, you know. But Hades—her husband—he can't come with her because he's stuck in hell, and stuff. But she comes back to hang out with her mom, and there are refreshments and everything at the dance... although really you shouldn't eat anything there. That can be dangerous."

"You want to talk about dangerous?" Darcy breaks in and Cassie turns to him with shining eyes. "Being a single male at Persephone's party. I was this close last year to becoming her summer boy toy." Darcy *is* cute, in a surfer dude kind of way. He has tanned skin and shaggy sun-kissed blonde hair.

"Oh no." Cassie reaches out and pats Darcy's arm. "She takes a boy every year," Cassie explains, turning back to me.

"I mean, we get them back in the fall, but they're just really dehydrated."

"Wow, the people in charge around here are a little predatory. Don't you think?" I say.

They all look back at me blankly. "Hermes flirted with me. Blatantly. Everyone knows Kratos is a little handsier than necessary when demonstrating a new move. And now we've got this Penelope chick terrifying all the boys."

"I wouldn't say we're terrified," Greg says, puffing out his bony little chest.

"No, we definitely are," Darcy says. "And I get what you're saying about the staff, but it's just sorta a different world here..."

"Not that different, unfortunately," I mutter.

Greg pokes me with his elbow. "You're being kind of a downer, Edie. Are you getting close to your breeding time of the month?"

I turn toward Greg and let out an exasperated little snort. We both jump when a hot puff of smoke comes from my nose.

Greg gulps. "I actually think that's kinda hot." He giggles. "Get it? Hot?"

Cassie must have a vision of me murdering Greg right here on the lunch table, because she leans toward Darcy and says in a too-loud voice, "You know, if you think it would help, I'd go to the dance with you." She smiles at Greg and me. "It could be a double date!"

Whoa. This is moving too fast.

"Or," I offer, "we can all ditch. That's what my friends and I did for the homecoming dance last year. We stayed in and watched horror movies and got take-out. It was the best homecoming ever."

They all stare at me like I have two heads.

"Nobody skips the Spring Fling," Cassie tells me.

Greg nods in agreement. "Attendance is mandatory."

"Really? I guess if it's a requirement..."

"Yay!" Cassie throws her hands up in the air. "Double dates." She reaches across the table to squeeze my hands. "I think this makes us sister wives. Right?"

Not for the first time I wonder who exactly is feeding Cassie's knowledge about the real world. "That's not what sister wives means."

"Sister friends then!?"

Just this once, I decide to let it go. "Yeah," I agree, squeezing back. "Sister friends."

"Edie," Darcy leans in, interrupting our sweet and slightly awkward moment. "Next time Cassie comes to the lagoon you should go with her. Maybe a nice relaxing soak will help you shift."

"Yeah, that sounds good," I tell him, touched he thought of me. I kinda get why Cassie is into him.

The bell chimes and we ditch our lunch trays. As we leave the dining hall I catch up to Fern.

"Hey, Edie. How's it going?" She looks genuinely pleased to see me. "I meant to check in with you but school has been crazy," she tells me.

"Oh, don't worry. Look," I pull her to the side. "There's a lot of gossip flying around about this bat shifter."

Her whole body stiffens and her face falls. "I don't know anything about that."

"I know what happened," I tell her, bluffing. "He didn't leave. He was injured."

She lets out a sigh and nods slightly. "They told us not to tell anyone. How do you know?"

"Mr. Zee." It's not a lie. I did learn it from him.

"It's such a shame," she confides, lowering her voice.

"There are so few bat shifters left and to have one just die unexpectedly..."

"Die?" I ask.

She nods. "His burns were horrible. We tried to save him but..."

"I'm sure you did all you could," I tell her, my mind racing. The bell rings again and Fern says she has to dash. I should really run too, but I'm lost in thought.

A student died and the Academy is trying to cover it up. Why?

16

A few hours later, Cassie and I are ready for action. Not wanting a repeat of last night, we're both dressed in all black. I may or may not have borrowed a few things from Tina's wardrobe (I totally did). Now we're creeping between buildings in a way that tells me maybe we should've sat in on a few of the Spying 101 classes before attempting this.

In short: our sneaking game is lame.

Finally, Cassie points across the way to a door I've never seen before at the side of the library. Probably because it's below ground level. "That's it," she whispers.

I nudge her. "You go first, just try to look casual. And then I'll come behind."

"Right." She nods and then walks very casually...on her tiptoes across the paved path.

She makes it across and I am slowly counting to ten when a voice whispers in my ear, "What are we doing right now?"

Somehow I keep the shriek from tearing out of my

throat. Only a little croak comes out instead. I whirl around and come face to face with Val.

"Oh," I say. And then hoping I'm better at faking casual than Cassie, I lean against the wall and ask, "Hey, what's up?"

He grins in that infuriatingly mocking way he has. "Not much. I just heard you were looking for me."

"That's ridiculous. Who told you that? It's not even a little bit true." It's totally true. I can't walk into a room or across campus without scanning it, wondering what t-shirt he's wearing today. It's a sickness.

Today it's a fluffy brown squirrel and says, *Who runs the world? Squirrels!*

"Hmm," he says. "I can't reveal my sources." He pauses as I glance toward the library door, hoping Cassie doesn't come running out calling my name. "So if you aren't out here hoping to bump into me during one of my famous midnight strolls, what exactly are you doing?"

I push away from the wall. "You are so arrogant. I don't know if you've noticed but there are tons of hot guys on this campus. Some of them are literal gods."

"Ah. So you've got your eye on one of our teachers, then."

"No! Of course not! Why does everyone think that's okay?" I give him a little shove, not for an excuse to touch his chest, but just to let him know I'm not intimidated. Of course, he just laughs and grabs hold of my hand, sandwiching it between two of his own.

"I wouldn't mind if you were looking for me." He voice is low and almost—but not quite—lacking that mocking edge. It's tempting to lean into him for a little late night necking. I could find out if the ice in his lips can withstand the fire behind my own.

But not tonight.

Not *any* night if I know what's good for me.

But definitely not when I am this close to getting answers about my family and maybe even what I am.

I jerk my hand away. "I know this may go against everything you believe about yourself, Val, but there are whole days that go by when I don't think about you."

"Whole days, huh?" His eyebrows lift. "Minutes. Maybe."

And then before I can think of a clever response—he's gone. Vampires do that a lot, moving so fast it's hard to keep up with them. Tina zips in and out of our room so fast that sometimes I don't even realize she's come and gone until I hear the squeak of a live mouse being slowly eaten by Vee in the corner.

After a moment, I remember this is what I wanted—to be able to go about my business without a hot vampire following me. Nice. Good choices, Edie.

Shoving both hands in my pockets (the one Val held still tingling with cold in a way that shouldn't be pleasant but somehow is) I saunter across the path and then after a quick glance assures me no one is around, quickly scurry down the steps to the lower library door. It's already opened a crack. I pull it just wide enough to slip through.

The hinges whine and I freeze, certain the whole campus can hear. But there is only quiet.

I step inside and shut the door behind me, leaving myself in darkness.

"Cassie?" I call.

"Not Cassie." A voice says next to me, and I totally scream, which makes her scream too.

"Shit!" I yell, falling to my feet. My arms pinwheel around me and I hit someone. There's the sound of papers falling, some of which flitter down in front of my face, immediately going up in flames.

Dammit, I'm setting things on fire again.

"Oh my god!" I say, as they turn in ashes in mid-air.

"Oh my *gods*," I'm corrected, by that same female voice. Suddenly, the lights are on and there's a woman standing over me, her brown hair in a long braid hanging over one shoulder. She holds a hand out to me.

"You must be Edie," she says, pulling me to my feet in one surprisingly strong yank. "Cassie has told me all about you."

"She has?" I ask, flustered. "Oh wait, are you her mom?"

"Yes," she nods. "Merilee Madges, hello."

"Hi," I say, brushing dirt off my butt to buy some time. Cassie's friend or not, I need to have a reason to be in the secret entranceway to the archives after hours. Cassie's face appears at her mom's shoulder, eyes large, mouth gaping, completely unhelpful.

"Cassie and I were hoping you could teach us more about—"

"Oh, yes, of course!" Merilee says, dropping the papers she had managed to hold onto. "I love when students take an interest in our records!"

She's so happy that someone wants to learn something she doesn't question us at all, simply takes both our hands and leads us down the corridor to her office, which appears to be called that only because it's four square feet of space without paper in it.

Stacks surround us. Literal stacks. I'm worried I'm going to knock something over and ruin everything, but Merilee doesn't seem concerned. She claims to be tidying as she walks, still talking to us, but there's no way she's doing anything right. She just jams papers in random places.

But I have to admit, she does it with confidence.

"Mom's filing system," Cassie says, beaming with pride. "They can't fire her because no one else understands it."

I remember Dad getting mad at Mom the one time she cleaned his maze of an office, claiming he couldn't find anything because she'd organized it. Sounds like Merilee figured out how to use her ability as a finder and ensure job security at the same time.

"So, girls," she says, licking the back of the last piece of paper and just sticking it to the wall. "What is it you want to know about?"

She'd been so excited about my use of the word *teach* earlier, it gave me time to come up with something.

"When I was at my other school we had an assignment in class, to look up world events in the year we were born and then write an essay about how those events have shaped our lives, even though we were just babies when they happened."

I toe the ground, appearing sheepish. "I thought, you know, since I'm having such a hard time fitting in, maybe if I did something similar, learned about what was happening at Mount Olympus in the year I was born, maybe I could start to understand how history has shaped this school, and find a way to..." I'm supposed to be lying, but I find tears in my eyes, anyway.

"Maybe you can find out if the world you really belonged in has shaped you, too?" Merilee asks, breathless, one hand on her heart. "Oh sweetheart, that's so..." She can't finish. She just hugs me.

"Nice," Cassie mouths at me.

"Alright, well..." Merilee wipes her eyes. "You're what, seventeen? Let me show you where some of the histories for that year would be."

"Some?" I ask, now jogging to keep up with her, Cassie at my heels.

"Well, yes, some," Merilee says. "Why would I keep them all in the same place?"

I don't answer, since she has this all figured out. Still, she didn't seem all that upset when I accidentally ashed a whole bunch of paper right in front of her. I wonder how much of her "I've got this" attitude is true, and how much is just an act.

What if she can't actually find what I need? What if— My wings pop out, knocking over two huge piles of paper on either side of us.

"I am so, so, sorry," I say, as pages lazily float down between us. "I just got a little nervous. It happens sometimes."

"Don't worry," Merilee says, plucking a paper from the air, reading it, then crushing it into a ball and throwing it over her shoulder.

My wings are a bright, iridescent blue at the moment, but the scales have a sheen to them, almost green with tinges of purple.

"Pretty," Cassie says, reaching out to touch them. I let her, but it doesn't feel nearly as nice as when Val did it. I was quaking so hard I thought I would drop all my scales, or catch him on fire again.

Wait. Holy shit.

"You guys," I grab Cassie's wrist, stopping her from stroking my wing. "I think I figured out what I am."

"Oh," Merilee says, casually slapping at the last piece of paper to fall. "This is exciting! Do tell!"

"I'm…" I swallow, looking from one face to the next. "I think I'm a dragon."

"Ohhhh...." Cassie says, then looks at her mom, whose eyes have gone super wide.

I feel a heat in my chest. "What? That's, like, something really special right? Like, rare?"

Merilee bursts into a snort, and Cassie starts giggling. She covers her mouth when I shoot her a dirty look, but tears are streaming out of her eyes.

"What?" I say, the heat in my chest changing to something more like irritation. "What'd I say?"

"Yeah, you're a dragon," she says, choking it out between laughs.

"And my boyfriend is a unicorn," Merilee says, which gets Cassie going all over again.

I cross my arms. "Okay, *what*?"

"You can't..." Merilee stops laughing, puts one hand on my arm. "Oh honey, I'm sorry, we're not trying to be mean. You can't be a dragon because those don't exist."

"What do you mean?" I insist. "Neither do werewolves and vampires and harpies!"

"Oh but they do," Merilee says. "But dragons..." She shakes her head. "Not a thing."

"Not a thing," Cassie agrees.

"Oh shut up," I snap at her. "You didn't know cell phones were a thing."

Merilee takes my arm, leading me further down the stacks of paper. "What we're trying to tell you is that there are only so many options when it comes to shifters. You can be a cat, a werewolf, an ostrich—"

"Seriously, still with that?"

She shrugs. "I don't make the rules. A bat," she continues. "But there aren't too many of those."

"I heard," I say, rolling my eyes and thinking of Greg.

"My guess is that you are a harpy," Merilee says, and I shudder thinking of Pity and her dry, withered body.

"A young harpy," Merilee continues. "We haven't had a new harpy in quite a long time; centuries, I would guess. I doubt anyone living today would remember what a young harpy looks like."

"But Pity tasted my blood," I say. "Ocypete," I clarify, when Merilee looks confused. "She said I'm not a harpy."

"Ah, well..." Marilee seems sad for a moment. "You have to realize that not everything in the human world and magical world is completely separate. Things like"—she lowers her voice—"*dementia* can still happen here."

"You're telling me Ocypete isn't all there?" I challenge her. Then I remember that my flying teacher cut her breasts off on purpose. It could be a fair assessment.

"Whatever," I say, slightly pissed that I'm wrong, and not a dragon.

"Don't be that way," Cassie says, touching my shoulder. Her eyes suddenly roll back into her head and she intones, "You will not have a very good time at Persephone's Spring Fling."

To her credit, Merilee rubs her daughter's back and smiles. "That's right, get it all out."

Luckily, Cassie's eyes haven't come back to the front in time to see me rolling my eyes at her lame prophecy.

"Great," she says, totally deflated. "As usual, I'm just saying dumb stuff. I mean, I know you're not going to have a good time at the Spring Fling. You're just going with Greg so that I can double with Darcy."

"Well..." I reach out, rubbing her hand. "I mean, yeah, that's true. But I wouldn't do it for anybody else. So look at it that way. My date is lame, but my best friend is awesome."

"Sister wives!" Cassie yells, then tries to high-five me,

misses completely and dives head first into three columns of paper that topple and fall on her.

"Sister wives?" Merilee asks. "I feel like I'm missing something."

"Join the club," I mumble as I help dig out Cassie. "I feel like I've missed all the things."

17

Merilee sends us on our way, directing us to the pile of files she says will have at least some of the history from the year I was born. She's "cleaning up" Cassie's mess—which appears to mean that she's tearing every third piece of paper into small pieces—when we walk away.

"I wasn't making fun of you, about the dragon thing," Cassie says, once we're out of earshot.

"You totally were," I tell her. "But it's okay. I can take a little teasing. And you still aren't getting what a sister wife is, by the way."

We settle in on the floor, surrounded by papers. Cassie starts in, pulling a random piece from the pile. "What am I looking for?"

"I don't know." I sigh. "Anything...weird?"

She nods. "Anything weird happening at the school for paranormal beings run by the gods who are at war with monsters, got it." And then she gets to work like it wasn't ironic at all. Which it probably wasn't meant to be.

I grab a paper too, scanning the words in front of me.

*And then Laurel said to Ivy that Uncas totally said I was
hotter than Pantha, which is totally true–*

"Hey, Cassie?" I ask. "When they say Archives and
Records..."

"Yep," she says, anticipating my question. "Anything
that's been written down, ever. I just found a janitor's list of
supplies."

"Great," I mutter. "This is going to be hell."

"Well," Cassie looks over her shoulder, lowers her voice.
"If we just told my mom we were looking for anything
having to do with your dad, she could find it right away.
That's what she does."

"I don't want to do that," I tell her. "What if it's something bad? Something she might feel she has to report? I
don't want to get your mom in any kind of trouble."

Plus, I am starting to wonder if Merilee is full of shit
with her finder thing. Like maybe Cassie's apple didn't fall
far from the tree in terms of gifts and abilities.

We read. And read. And read some more.

I learn about crushes and breakups from almost two
decades ago. Notes from a class that's no longer taught—
Trees That Will Eat You—because apparently they are
extinct now.

"Dragons don't exist, my ass," I say under my breath,
then grab another paper.

I had been clicking my tongue, biding my time as I read,
but suddenly, I go very still.

*Student Daniel Evans fled the grounds last night. He carries
with him two secrets that could ruin the Academy forever, if their
existence was known. Steps must be taken.*

"Cassie," I whisper. "I've found something."

She comes to my side, reads over my shoulder, then
shakes her head. "No, you didn't."

"What do you mean?" I snap. "It says my dad's name right there! He learned two secrets and he ran away. We've got to find out what they were!"

But Cassie is still shaking her head. "It's not him. Look," she points to the date at the top of the page. "The year is totally wrong. It's the year you were born and students can't have kids. There's too much magic flying around here to ensure the safety of the fetus, and the mother. If you get pregnant you're done, off campus."

"Yeah, but just the girls, right?" I ask, insistent, but Cassie shakes her head. "Why not?"

"Shifters and vamps have had bad blood for, like, ever," Cassie says. "Ages ago the vamps wanted to whittle down the student body, get rid of as many shifters as they could, but they wanted to have some fun, too, right? So the vamp bros got a bunch of shifter girls pregnant, told them they'd had a spell cast on them that makes them shoot blanks."

"But they didn't?" I guessed. "That's awful!"

"Yeah, so a whole bunch of girls got pregnant, and the shifters were all pissed. They insisted that the fathers be punished too." Cassie shakes her head. "It was a small graduating class that year. So anyway, yeah, Daniel Evans can't be your dad, because he was a student when you were born, and they take the pregnancy law very seriously."

Cassie doesn't notice that my hand is shaking, or that I have goosebumps.

"I mean," she goes on, "like they take it *super* seriously. Hermes made one of the magical instructors come up with this truth serum that they used on all the dudes, to make them spill if they were the fathers. So there's no way Daniel Evans is your dad. Unless...oh my gods!"

She gasps, her arm on my shoulder. I think she just figured it out.

"Unless you're not actually seventeen. Cassie, is it possible that you're..." She gulps. "Thirteen?"

"Or..." I can't help but recall Cassie's prophecy from last night. About my father not being the one I want. You can't unhear shit like that. It's been running through the back of my mind in an ugly loop pretty much nonstop. "Maybe my dad isn't really my dad."

"Oh..." Cassie says, then takes a second to think about it. "Ohhhhhhhhhh. Well, I mean, either way—you still want to know what the secrets are, right?"

"Yeah," I say, getting up. It's hard because there are tears in my eyes, and my knees are shaky. I start down a random corridor of papers, Cassie in my wake.

"Hey," she says, plucking at my wrist. "It could totally be the wrong guy, right? Like Daniel Evans is a super common name. There could have been two Daniel Evans at the school."

I let hope rise in my chest. "Yes," I agree. "I guess so."

"Here," she says confidently. "We'll ask Mom." She raises her voice before I can tell her not to. "Mooooommm!! We have a question."

Merilee is at our side immediately, whipping her braid around to the other shoulder. "Yes?"

"Has there ever been more than one Daniel Evans enrolled at Mount Olympus Academy?" Cassie asks her mom.

"Let me check," Merilee says, and I'm about to say no, that I'm done, that I don't want to go traipsing through more piles of paper, when Merilee's eyes roll back into her head. She's like that for a few seconds, then they come back to the front.

"No," she says. "One Daniel Evans only."

"What???" I'm so confused I don't have time to be disappointed about my paternity.

"Mom retains everything she reads," Cassie says, resting her head on Merilee's shoulder. "To the letter."

"Wow," I say, impressed. "So all of this..." I gesture to the piles of paper around me.

"Just for show, really." Merilee shrugs, and taps her temple. "It's all up here."

"But what if you quit?" I ask. "Or...get struck by lightning and end up in a coma?"

Merilee laughs. "Don't say something like that! Not on this campus."

"Oh, gods. Sorry!" I try to back pedal but Merilee waves me off.

"It's okay. I'm just teasing. But to answer your question, I can pass on my gift—it's a simple spell. It's willed to Cassie right now. She'll always have a place here. I'll make sure of that."

"Nice," I say.

But the sight of Merilee stroking Cassie's head, and the light in my friend's eyes as she looks up at her mom takes all the breath out of me. They're so happy. So close. So proud of each other. Such a family.

Like the one that was taken from me.

Or at least...who I thought was my family.

18

My head is reeling from what we found out about my father. I don't even know where to start. Is my dad not actually my dad? Or did he have me and Mavis in secret? But if he was here, where and when did he meet my mom? So many questions.

In hand-to-hand combat, Cassie and I are trying to knock each other off balance and are basically having a slap fight.

"Val!" Kratos yells across the room. "Help the new girls. They're pathetic."

Cassie raises her hand. "Mr. Kratos, I really have to pee. That UTI I saw has arrived in full force and…"

"Just go." Mr. Kratos shakes his head.

"No way." Tina marches over and plants herself in front of Kratos. "The last time *this one* worked with Val she set him on fire. He is not working with her again."

I wait for Tina's Greek chorus of friends to chime in, but they hang back, watching silently.

Kratos doesn't say a word. He simply shifts his weight in such a way that he goes from casually standing to an aggressive stance that communicates, *this is the last thing you will see before you die.*

Um, why aren't they teaching us that in class?

I gotta give Tina credit. I'm ready to roll on my belly and it's not even directed at me. Tina, though, just sorta sniffs and with her head held high mutters, "Whatever," and walks away. Somehow she makes sure her path goes directly through where I'm standing. She roughly elbows me aside, while hissing, "You'll pay for this."

It's such a stereotypical villain line, I can't help but add, "Yeah, and my little dog too, right?"

She rolls her eyes. "Why would I care about your dog, you freak?"

"Back to work," Kratos calls. He jerks his chin in my direction. "Don't set anyone on fire."

"Well, that was fun," Val says as he saunters toward me. Today he's wearing a shirt with a guy in an office wearing an astronaut suit that says, *Dress for the job you want.*

My heart is still pounding from the stress of it all. "I really thought for a few minutes there that I wasn't going to have roommate problems anymore."

Val laughs, low and throaty. "Yeah, if it was anyone else, maybe Kratos would've taken their head off. But Tina's not an idiot. She knows being top of our class means she gets a little more leeway than everyone else."

"Top of the class?" I glance her way where she's once again surrounded by friends. I've been so busy trying to survive my classes I haven't really paid much attention to Tina, except trying to stay out of her way. But now that I think about it, the teachers are constantly praising her, or using her for demos, or giving her what I've come to know as the highest compliment of all for those of us in the assassination class, "NBK, Tina."

I had to ask Cassie what NBK meant. She, of course, giggled as she explained, "Natural born killer."

"Tina's always been competitive," Val says now. "And since she doesn't like anyone except herself and me, stepping on others to get what she wants has never been a problem."

He says this affectionately, like it's an annoying yet charming character trait similar to snorting when you laugh.

"And what about you?" I ask.

Val raises a single eyebrow. "Are you asking if I like you?"

Ugh. I blush and hate myself for getting bothered as I quickly correct, "I meant, are you competitive?"

We reach the mats. Val immediately moves into a fighting crouch and I do the same.

"Nah. I've never been into the whole Academy thing. I wouldn't even stay here if it wasn't for Tina."

This surprises me so much that I forget to defend and Val's super slow punch connects with my shoulder. I stumble back a step.

"New girl, focus up!" Kratos yells, while I rub my shoulder.

"Sorry," Val says, "I thought you were ready."

"My fault, I was daydreaming." I go back into fighting stance and this time manage to block most of Val's punches...although that's mostly because he's practically moving in slow motion. If I had any pride I'd tell him to pick it up a little, but the truth is, I already can feel a bruise forming where he connected with my shoulder.

And also my mind just isn't in the game. Hearing Val say he doesn't want to be here, makes me reevaluate everything I've seen of him.

He tends to hang at the edge of class. Not really

mingling with the vampires unless Tina makes him. Just now when Kratos called him over to work with me, he was leaning against the wall, just sort of watching. I always assumed it was because he's so good he doesn't need these classes. Like he's just above it all.

Now though, I realize with blinding clarity—he's an outcast too.

When I burned him, Tina was upset. But the others were surprisingly quiet.

Same with just now. Tina wanted to keep Val away from me, but her friends looked like they'd be happy for me to BBQ him again.

The other vamps don't like him. Or trust him. Maybe because of his roommate best friend from last year? I want to ask, but...

Val sidles up to me and in one swoop has me pinned on the mat. He's on top of me but being very careful not to put too much pressure on my body. His barely touching sends a tingle through me and I shiver.

Our eyes meet and I can tell he's about to say something important. Meaningful even. Possibly a declaration of love. Which would be a little too much, a little too soon...but maybe I could roll with it.

"Edie," he says, his voice deep and rumbling through me where our bodies connect. "You're the worst fighter in this class. By like, a lot."

I gasp. Putting my hands on Val's chest, I push. He doesn't budge. "Get off me."

"I don't even think you're trying."

"You're bigger than me!"

"I mean, in class. You're holding back." Val rolls away.

Slowly, I sit up. I don't look at Val, but I can feel him beside me. My throat is tight, almost like I'm going to cry.

It is a small point of pride that I have not actually broken down in tears in the middle of class yet. I am not going to let Val ruin that streak.

"I'm not the worst," I say. And then, feeling guilty, I add, "What about Cassie?"

Val shrugs. "Cassie tries. She gives it her all."

This really stings. I also hate that Pity said something similar the other day. I spring to my feet. "So do I! I give one hundred percent."

He shakes his head. "No, you're holding back. Always. You're afraid."

Val stands, the movement liquid smooth. Somehow we are face to face, with barely an inch between us. His finger taps at my chest. Once. Twice. Mimicking the rhythm of my heart. "You're afraid of whatever's in there. Afraid of letting it out."

I close my eyes. The thing inside me stares back. Almost like it's taunting me. Or daring me to let it loose.

My eyes burst open again.

Okay, maybe I am a little bit afraid.

"That sounds about right," Kratos booms into my ear.

I jump, springing away from Val.

Hands on hips, legs spread wide, Kratos nods knowingly. "A shifter that doesn't shift is like a person that doesn't shit. You're constipated."

Tina and her crowd go crazy over this. "I knew she was full of shit," Tina tells her cronies.

Val is, as usual, inscrutable.

Still determined not to cry in class, I ball my hands into fists and run from the room. If I can get outside before the tears start, it won't count.

Who am I kidding? I am once again humiliated.

19

I keep running until I make it to a copse of trees and then collapse on my knees, burying my face in my hands. I expect to cry, or at least be out of breath, but my asthma hasn't acted up at all since I've been here. I take a deep breath and prepare for a sob, except now that I'm here, nothing comes out.

Maybe I'm emotionally constipated too. A shaky laugh comes out of me at this thought.

"That's the right attitude," Val says. Even without seeing him, I already know his voice too well.

Also, no one else sneaks with quite his level of finesse.

"Can I just have thirty seconds of privacy?" I ask, not bothering to lift my face from my hands.

"I wanted to apologize. I didn't mean for our conversation to go that way."

"You mean Kratos didn't put you up to it?" I imitate his voice, "Val, give the new girl a talking to."

Val laughs. "You really think Kratos would instruct me to have a heart to heart with you?"

Finally, I turn around and look at him. "Heart to heart? Is that what it was?"

Val looks away first. He tilts his head back to study the branches overhead. "It's not any of my business, but you're obviously struggling with the whole shifter thing and it doesn't seem like anyone's really helping you figure it out."

"But I thought shifting is just something you're supposed to know how to do. Like breathing."

Val shakes his head. "That's not what Derrick said. He was surprised we didn't have meditation classes here. His whole family made it part of their daily routine. A way to stay in touch with their inner beast."

For half a second I imagine myself attempting to sit in lotus position and "ohm" my way to some sort of relationship with the glowing-eyed monster inside me. Then I imagine Tina walking in and laughing her ass off, maybe leaving me in a meditative state long enough to let Vee bite off one of my ears.

So yeah, that's not gonna happen.

I decide to focus on the roommate part of Val's story instead.

I hesitate, not sure if I should ask, but unable to resist. "Derrick...wasn't he your old roommate? The traitor who ran away?"

Val's face goes dark and his eyes get fiery in a way that makes me realize anew how dangerous he is. "Everyone has secrets, Edie. This is about yours. The ones you're keeping from yourself. Doesn't it seem like the school almost prefers that you don't figure it out? Like it's easier for everyone if what you are stays inside?"

This gets my attention. "*They* who?"

"The administration, the gods. You know how it is around here."

"Actually, I don't." I stand, much less gracefully than Val. "I've been here two months and every day I learn something new that supposedly is common knowledge. I had to get a book of Greek mythology from the library to learn about our teachers. And I still haven't met Mr. Zee who's supposedly in charge of this whole place."

Val frowns. "Really? Zee didn't make a point of greeting you on your first day? Shaking your hand and all that?"

"No."

"Well, maybe he just does that for the vampires. It's kind of a big deal that we're here."

"It is?" I throw my hands up. "See? I don't know anything."

Val smiles. "That's actually not well known. I think they've tried to keep it under wraps. It's all tied up in vampire clan politics, which everyone finds boring."

I shake my head, wondering if I'll ever get used to living in a world where vampire politics are referred to as 'boring.'

"That sounds interesting to me," I say.

"It's not. The clan I'm part of made a deal with the gods to send their young to the Academy, in return for various favors and protections."

"So you didn't have a choice?"

He shoves his hands in his pockets as his face goes dark, like he's mentally shutting himself off. "There are always choices," he says at last. "Just not always good ones."

"Yeah, I get that. But what about living with your choices? Hermes gave me all of two seconds to decide if I wanted to come here and then I was just thrown in. Most of the time I'm working so hard not to get left behind I don't think about it, but sometimes, when I pause for a minute, it's just like, 'what am I even doing here?' And I remember home and I just...miss things, you know?"

I'm sniffing now, holding back a good cry. Where the hell is this coming from? I haven't even said these things to Cassie.

"Like what?" Val asks. "What do you miss?"

"Okay, so," I look up at the sky. "We're still in Florida, right? But it never rains here. I actually liked that. I liked the rain. I...I miss it."

I wipe a tear away, but wait...it's not a tear. It's cold, and... I lick it off my finger. Not salty. "Wait," I look up, and there is the smallest dark raincloud right above my head, cool drops falling around me in a circle.

I look at Val, who is watching the cloud with a soft smile. He does not look at all mystified by this unexplainable weather phenomenon. The moment he notices me watching him, Val closes up again, the softness melting away—along with the cloud over my head. I look up and there's no trace of it. If I wasn't soaking wet, I would've thought it was my imagination.

"What was that?" I ask.

Val shrugs. "You must have some sort of wish-granting abilities. You asked for rain, and you got it."

"I'm pretty sure I didn't do that," I say, watching him closely as I pull my wet hair up into a ponytail.

"Let me help," Val says. His hands brush my neck, and I jump away, both loving and hating the shiver that passes through me at his touch.

"I better get back to class. Cassie will be looking for me."

"Right." He nods, once again looking smug and above it all. It's hard to tell if this is a mask or the real Val.

As I push through the trees and make my way back towards the training rooms, Val falls into step beside me.

"I heard you're going with Greg to the Spring Fling."

I miss a step and Val grabs my elbow to keep me from falling on my face. "Where did you hear that?"

"Greg is telling anyone who will listen."

I groan.

"I hear it's a double date too." Val laughs and it is not at all like the nice laugh he uses when I say something funny. This is a mean one that reminds me of his sister.

I throw my shoulders back and stick my nose in the air. "For your information, Greg is a lovely boy and a delightful...bat. It's very possible I might be a bat too and so it seems natural for the two of us—"

"You're not a bat." Val cuts me off. He says this like it's an irrefutable fact.

"Okay, fine. I'm going with Greg regardless. And Cassie and Darcy too. We're going to have a wonderful double date time." I do not believe this in the slightest, but there's no way I'm admitting it to Val.

"Okay," he says mildly. "I'm sure you will."

This response is aggravating for reasons I can't quite put my finger on. Simmering, I ask, "And what about you?"

"No double dates for me. Vampires don't double date."

"Don't or won't?" It's almost impossible to keep track of all the various traditions and superstitions surrounding the various creatures here.

"Don't," Val repeats, turning to me with a slight smile warming his eyes. "Double dates are a lot like holy water. They won't kill us, but can still cause a lot of pain."

I laugh then, unable to resist. And Val joins in.

It's a nice, non-tense moment that's interrupted by a terrible screeching noise.

"That's the alarm," Val yells over the horrible sound. "Something is wrong."

We hurry over to where the rest of our class is pouring out of the practice rooms.

"Everyone, calmly make your way outside," Kratos calls out. The vamps don't seem very concerned. That is until we make it to the quad and notice the crowd surrounding a pile of ash.

Tina pushes through everyone and actually begins to sob.

"What is happening?" I ask no one.

Tina pulls a metal object from the ash. "This is Jenn's nose-ring. She never takes it off!" She screams. "This is Jenn!"

Oh shit. One of Tina's crew forgot her sunscreen? Seems unlikely. She turns to me. "This is your fault, you bitch!"

Wait. What? I look behind me. There's a mousy cat-shifter who has only ever managed to look like an alley cat with mange, and I'm pretty sure she's not a bitch. Great. Tina's definitely talking to me.

Themis comes running over the grass, skirt stretching against her quads, high heels held in one hand. Val is at Tina's side, pulling her away. I wait for him to tell everyone I was with him the whole time, but he doesn't say a word.

"I didn't..." I don't understand.

"Don't deny it," Tina shouts. "Who else is going around setting people on fire?"

"Everyone needs to return to their dorms at once," Themis declares in a voice as loud as a bullhorn, not out of breath even after her run.

People begin to turn away, some giving me looks, but I'm rooted in place. That pile of ash is a murdered person and... and I'm suspect number one?

Themis turns to me. "Ms. Evans, please come to my office at once."

"I didn't do this," I tell her, desperately. "I wouldn't."

"We can discuss that in my office."

Val continues leading Tina away but she's still shouting, "You'll get what you deserve, you dirty shifter."

Cassie appears at my side. "Hey...what did I miss?"

20

"There is absolutely no proof that Ms. Evans hurt anyone," Themis tells the assembled school. We're in an outdoor amphitheater, I guess what Mount Olympus Academy uses as an auditorium. As much as I try to hide in the back, the whole of the student body is sneaking looks at me. For the first time, I'm thrilled we can't have cell phones. I'd be viral by now.

I barely pay attention, even though she's talking about me. I know that I didn't hurt anyone, but Tina is right, I totally could have. Whatever is inside me, whatever I shift into, I think it's probably pretty scary. All the more reason for me to keep it locked inside.

I tune back in to Themis. "I brought her to my office not because she was under suspicion, but because I feared a few of her classmates might have the wrong idea and try to take vengeance into their own hands."

Yeah, no doubt the vamps would break their no-biting-shifters rule for me. I catch Tina's glare. Val sits beside her, not looking at me at all. Maybe our flirtation ends here.

"Believe me, the tragic death of Jennifer LaMont will not go unpunished. Please, leave this in the hands of the faculty and staff. We will get to the truth of the matter. Justice will be served. Any attempts made by students to deliver retribution, or deal with the matter themselves, will not only hinder our investigation, but bring the utmost punishment upon them."

"If anyone feels the need to talk to me, I will be available with one of our medics skilled in grief counseling. Ms. LaMont's family will be on campus later. This is a sad time for them, so please do not exacerbate the situation with unfounded accusations. Now, everyone. Return to class. They will continue as scheduled."

"See," Cassie tells me. "No one actually thinks you hurt Jenn."

"Tina does." I turn to her. "Can't you see who did it?" I ask, jumping to my feet.

"That's not how being a seer works. I can see the future, not the past." We walk down the stone steps and out of the amphitheater.

I deflate. "Well, I'd better get to my flying tutorial. I don't want to be stuck walking alone with the vamps out for blood."

"No one is going to hurt you..." Cassie says, somewhat breezily. "Didn't you hear Themis? The *utmost punishment*... that means like..."

She breaks off, suddenly without words. I turn, ready to catch her if she's going into another trance and is going to rant about monsters doing jazz hands again. Instead she's just quiet, pensive, her brow furrowed.

"Means what?" I nudge her. "The utmost punishment is what?"

"At Mount Olympus traitors are punished by flood or fire. Sometimes they even get a choice."

"Drown or burn?" I ask, and Cassie nods. I shiver, not knowing which I'd choose. "Wait," I go on. "Does this mean that Jenn was a traitor? Why was *she* burned?"

"I doubt it," Cassie shakes her head. "They would make a big show out of killing a traitor, get Mr. Zee involved and everything. Speaking of which, where the hell is he? Themis always ends up doing all the work, poor woman. Last year, after that student turncoat took off, it was Themis who went after her. I mean, men, am I right?"

I let Cassie go on until she runs out of steam, then bring the conversation back to the original point—my safety. "I appreciate what Themis said, but I'm not going to take any chances. Vamps don't like following the rules, right?"

Greg and Darcy wait for us at the exit, along with Fern. "Tough break," Darcy says. "I mean, someone gets murdered by burning and you're notorious for starting random fires…"

"I didn't do it," I tell them.

"No, of course not," Fern says.

"I didn't think you did," Greg tells me, staring at the ground. "Though Jenn was a total bitch. I mean, not to talk ill of the dead but she once told me that the legend about vamps turning into bats was true. She said we were fated to mate, and I was like—awesome. I can contribute to society and bang a hot chick, right? So, she told me to meet her in the ruins so we could mate, then surprised me with her whole vampire crew when I had my pants down." He looks up at me. "Hmmm, I feel like this is one of those oversharing moments that Darcy is always telling me about."

"Yeah, it definitely is." Darcy chimes in.

"TMI," Fern agrees.

I shake my head. "Look, I'm late. Ocypete is going to kill me." I put my hand over my mouth. "Poor choice of words."

Darcy nods. "I'm heading to the lagoon—"

"I'll join you!" Cassie says very loudly. Darcy gives her a shy grin. I can't help but smile.

"How dare you smile when my best friend is dead," Tina yells at me. She is flanked by her vampire goonies. I expect Val to...well, maybe not defend me, but at least shepherd her away. Instead he just stands at her side looking moody.

"Drop it, Tina," Fern tells her.

"No one asked you, you witchy bitch."

"Tina!" One of her crew objects, the first time I've ever seen any of them speak out about her. Tina turns on the girl with fire in her eyes.

"Don't get me started on you, Marguerite. I know you and Fern have a thing going on. Don't you dare take her side."

Marguerite looks cowed and Fern shrinks back. Are relationships between the disciplines that taboo? Or is it just good old-fashioned interspecies bigotry?

Back in charge, Tina again turns her wrath on me. She stalks forward, teeth exposed.

"Break it up!" Ocypete drops in between us like a stone, her claws flashing, body curled and ready to strike.

"We were just talking," Tina tells her defiantly.

"Well, stop talking and start walking to your next class or I'm going to put a few slash marks on your pretty little face. And I'll tell the medics no blood for you for a week."

"You wouldn't!" Tina cries out.

"Try me."

Ocypete gives a half lunge towards her and Tina retreats, stumbling over a tree root and landing on her butt. Vampires are always graceful, so seeing one of their own down in the dirt is shocking enough to elicit a giggle from her own crew, which makes Tina even angrier.

Tina throws out a hand and Val immediately helps her up, like a trained dog.

"She killed my friend," she yells at Ocypete, and I'm surprised to see her lower lip trembling. "She started it!"

"And I'm ending it!" Ocypete roars, her old woman voice suddenly inflated as her wings come out full span. She spins, making eye contact with the whole crowd. "Edie is off limits. Get to your classes. NOW!"

Everyone scatters, including Darcy, Cassie, and Greg. I don't blame them. Harpies are seriously scary.

Ocypete looks at me. "Well, come on. You're not going to learn to fly on your own."

We make our way to the practice field.

"Thanks," I say. "I really didn't hurt that vampire. I didn't even know her. When I burned Val it was an accident. I wouldn't just kill someone randomly for no reason."

"I know you wouldn't. Elysa wouldn't have raised someone so heartless."

"Wait." I stop and stare. "You knew my grandmother?"

"Look, there is a lot you don't know, about your parents, about you..." She glances around.

"Well, tell me!" I demand.

"It's not safe to talk here." She motions past the practice field. "My nest is about half a mile that way, in a giant cypress. You have to fly to get there."

"Let's go!" I flap my wings and manage to get a few feet off the ground before crashing back down. Ocypete studies me.

"You're not ready yet. Not to fly and not to learn the truth."

I want to cry, but it won't help anything. Ocypete isn't going to budge.

"Let's get on with our lesson," she tells me, not unkindly. "Let's treat it as an incentive. Once you can fly to my nest, I'll tell you what I know."

I stand, more determined than ever. There are answers out there, and I need to find the truth.

21

I don't want to go to my room, not with Tina waiting to avenge Jenn's death, so I make my way back down to the archives. Merilee smiles at me.

"Cassie saw that you'd be back without her. She asked me to help you. You've been such a good friend to her. She's never really fit in, despite being raised here. I'm grateful to you."

"Then you'll help me?" I ask, relieved.

"If I can. I keep the official records of the Academy. I'm not privy to everything, though. The gods like to have their secrets."

"At this point, I'll take what I can get." I sit down, unsure how honest to be. "You said Cassie has a hard time fitting in. Well, I'm the same way. I don't know how to fly, or how to shift, or even what I should be shifting into!"

I try not to notice that Merilee has covered her mouth, obviously still amused at the fact that I thought I could be a dragon.

"I'm so far behind everyone else, I don't belong here. But I don't belong back home, either." Merilee reaches out and touches my arm lightly, the way she touched Cassie the other night, like a mother. It brings tears to my eyes. "My dad is gone, and he took a lot of secrets with him—secrets about my past. The other night I wasn't working on an assignment—please don't be mad."

Merilee's mouth goes into a thin line but she nods at me to continue.

"Cassie was trying to help me find out more about my father...Daniel Evans."

Her eyes go wide when I say his name, linking it with my own. "Oh..." She pushes some hair out of her face, her hand shaking a little. "I didn't realize."

"Merilee, I need you to tell me everything you know about my father," I say.

She looks around, as if afraid there might be someone in the archives with us. Finally, when she is satisfied we are alone, her eyes roll back in her head. "Daniel Evans. Parentage unknown. Was found in the marsh by the school as an infant. Raised by Themis. Was on the magical track when he absconded with a student, Layla Larchmere."

"Wait, my parents met here?" I interrupt. "My mom was a...?"

"Witch," Merilee comes back to herself. "A talented one, one of our best healers. When they left, it was a scandal."

"But there's some secret that they took with them. The other night in the archives I found a reference to him leaving with secrets—two of them..." I stop, thinking hard. "Wait, if Dad ran off with Mom the same year I was born, and if the two little secrets were me and my sister, she couldn't have given birth to us because she wouldn't have been allowed to be pregnant on campus...

"Oh my gods," I mutter. "My mom's not my mom, either, is she?"

Merilee sighs. "There is something...this is not in the records. I came back from my own sabbatical, just having had Cassandra, when I received a delivery of baby clothes. But I hadn't ordered them. They were brought to me because I had Cassie but the name on the box was...they were for Themis."

I shake my head. "My sister and I were raised in secret by Themis? Is she my mother?" My head is spinning.

"I don't think you can assume that," Merilee says. "After all, Themis raised your father from an infant, and he's certainly not her child. Themis just has a soft spot for unwanted children. Oops." She claps her hand over her mouth, eyes wide and guilty.

"Unwanted?" I repeat, tears brewing.

"I wish I could help you more," Merilee tells me. "But at least I think you figured out the two secrets your dad escaped with."

"Yeah." I have to agree, but it doesn't feel like a victory. Far from it. Especially when the answers only lead to more questions.

Why did Mom and Dad take us? Were we in danger? Was Themis trying to harm us? Or were we just not safe here?

And the biggest question of all...who the Hades are my real parents?

My excuse to see Themis is that I want a room change. I can't sleep in the same room with Tina, and who knows whatever vamps may try to kill me in my sleep. While I'm waiting in the hall, I hear crying in her office. After a few minutes two people leave; both look to be in their twenties and like they could be models if it weren't for their stricken expressions.

"Ms. Evans." Themis motions me inside.

"Were those Jenn's parents?" I ask.

"They were." She sits, cradles a cup of tea with her hands.

"That's so sad. How does that work...with vampires?" I ask.

Themis looks at me. "I forget how little you know. Vampires are ageless, yes, and can be turned from humans, but they can also be born. They grow as normal humans do until they reach maturity. Usually around their twenty-fifth year or so." She takes a sip of tea.

"Oh. That makes sense." We stare at each other for a moment longer before I ask, "So...are you my birth mother?"

Themis spits out her tea. "I...no...who told you that?"

"No one. But I know there is something you're not telling me. About my past."

Themis stands, but she seems shaky. I definitely flustered her.

"Ms. Evans, I know you've had a hard day but I do not have time for this insanity. And I advise you *not* to go around asking every instructor on campus if they are your mother. That could be...dangerous."

"I just want to know the truth," I protest.

"Yes, I understand. But sneaking around the archives with Cassandra may not be the best way to achieve your objectives." I open my mouth to argue again, but she holds up a single finger, letting me know she's not done. "A large part of who you are lives inside you, but your professors tell me you're no closer to shifting than you were on day one. In fact, they believe you're holding back."

The finger falls, but I have nothing to say in my defense.

Themis nods. "I know you will not be happy to hear this, but it has been decided that if you have not shifted by the weekend of the Persephone's Spring Fling, you will be moved to another discipline effective immediately."

"But that's two weeks away!" I stand and my wings billow out behind me.

"A shift takes mere seconds. And you've had more than enough time."

With a hand on my back, she ushers me toward the door. "You may want to take some time over these next few weeks and think about which other discipline might be a better fit for you."

"I don't want another discipline," I say as she shuts the door in my face.

"Thanks. Great talk," I tell the thick door.

22

"Earth to Edie," Cassie says. "Where is your head at?"

"Oh...nowhere. Here. I guess."

I'm bunking in Cassie's room despite not getting permission. I've had enough of Tina and her little shop of horrors. Her vamp roommate is still shacking up with her boyfriend so her bed is free. Cassie is beyond delighted. She's in full sleepover mode, talking non-stop about Darcy, and the dance, and dancing with Darcy. It's hard to focus when I have so many questions and not nearly enough answers.

"Hey, is your roommate worried about getting pregnant?" I ask.

"Super random, but no. There's a spell for that."

"Does it work one hundred percent of the time? I mean, I don't know how much you know about birth control in the real world, but it's not a fail safe."

"Are you thinking about...you're not going to have sex with Greg, are you?"

"Oh, gods no! I'm just curious."

"Well, it's pretty effective...just not if you're boinking an actual god. God sperm is like—" She does jazz hands. "You and Greg should be fine."

"I'm not boinking Greg!" I yell, throwing a pillow at her. "But what about you and Darcy? Have you gotten the magical birth control spell put on you?"

"Darcy?" She blushes bright red. "No, we're not there yet. I do like him, though."

"Yeah, I can tell."

"He dropped one of his scales for me. I think it was one of those accidentally on purpose things." She reaches inside her drawer and pulls out a gigantic shiny aqua fish scale.

"Wait, Cassie," I say, a smile brewing on my lips. "When he goes into the water and turns into a merman, does he have his pants on?"

"Um..." She bites her lip. "No."

"And you're there?" I push.

"I..." She blushes. "I don't look. That would be rude. Not that they care, really. I swear the merfolk are the most immodest of all the shifters." She goes a deeper shade of red.

I laugh and she throws a pillow at me, but only lightly, still holding fast to the iridescent scale in her hand.

"That, like, came from his body?" I ask, a bit grossed out.

"Yeah but..." She stops, and her eyes roll back in her head. I expect her to see what will be for breakfast tomorrow or tell me something about the weather. What she does say chills me to my core.

"The water born boy will lose his head on the night of the spring celebration. A child of the gods will take flight and destroy one she loves. Flames shall rain from the heavens and the monsters shall cry in fear."

Cassie comes back to herself. "Holy shit."

"Cassie," I ask, my goosebumps settling, "are you okay?"

"No, I..." She shakes her head. "Oh my gods, Edie...that didn't feel good."

"Yeah." I smile at her, trying to calm her down. "It's always a little weird when you go into a trance."

"No, I mean, the whole thing felt different. Like, what I said wasn't about tuna, or foot fungus, or cheating on a test. That one felt important. That one felt real."

"Is this the first one that felt like that?"

"Yes," she nods. "But ever since I touched that Seer Stone I've felt a little different, a little off. Like something was building up inside me. And now this?"

She hiccups. "I just tried to ignore it. I think so many people have told me my abilities are lame that I started to believe it. I never thought I'd ever really see something important, Seer Stone or not."

"Oh, Cassie." I reach over and rub her back while also feeling guilty as hell. I definitely never thought she'd see something important either. But saying that isn't going to help, so instead I concentrate on the prophecy.

"Okay. You said a water born boy would lose his head at the Spring Fling."

Her brow furrows, thinking. "I touched Darcy's scale and then...oh no. Edie! He's going to die at the dance!"

I tighten my arm around her. "You don't know that," I say. "You said *the water born boy*, not specifically him. It could be any merman...it could be the Leviathan, that awful thing that killed my dad. He definitely looked water born."

She shakes her head. "No, it was Darcy's scale that made me go into a trance. The vision is connected to him. But how do I tell him? Everyone thinks my visions are a total joke."

"Cassie..." I don't know how to put it without being offensive. "How sure are you about this? You can lose your head in a lot of different ways. Maybe he just gets angry at something. You really don't want to start your relationship off by telling Darcy he's going to die and then have it not happen, right?"

"Uh, so it's better to tell him he's going to die and actually have him die, so he goes to the afterlife knowing I'm not a fraud?" Cassie asks, and we both burst out laughing.

"Okay, okay, no. Scratch that," I agree. "What I mean is, what if you tell him he's going to die and he doesn't?"

No longer laughing, Cassie says, "But what if I don't warn him, and he *does*?"

"Wow," I say, processing her problem. "Well, just try to find a good time to tell him? I mean, you've got to find a nice way to let him know that he might die...nicely. Like, not over breakfast."

"You're so right," Cassie quickly agrees. "Lunch would be better, right?"

"No. Not at lunch. And definitely don't compare this prophecy to the tuna noodle casserole vision either." Surely that's more offensive to the merfolk than a regular person.

"Not lunch, not breakfast...what about dinner? Good time, you think? Maybe?"

I turn out the light. "Good night, Cassie."

"So not during meal time at all?"

23

W e're woken in the middle of the night by alarms wailing. Cassie and I smash into each other as we scramble from our beds, still half asleep. Cassie puts her hand on the doorknob and screams, clutching it to her chest.

"It's scalding," she tells me, coughing.

I grab a shirt and try the knob, but I can't get it turned. Finally I just use my hands. It's hot, but not painful. I look down at my palm and purple scales glisten back at me. Something tugs inside of me, similar to how it feels before I let my wings out. I have a feeling with just a little push, I could shift. Right here. Right now.

I ball both hands into fists and hold it back. Even with the threat of being kicked out of the Assassination Class—I'm still not ready.

Cassie taps my shoulder. "Are we waiting for something?"

I blink and realize I've been standing here while the building burns down around us. There's no time for this right now.

"Sorry!" I throw the door open.

The hallway is full of smoke, and Cassie falls to her knees. "The air is clearer near the floor," she shouts.

I'm not having any trouble breathing so I lead the way and drag Cassie beside me. We crawl through the thick smoke until we reach the stairwell. Thankfully, the smoke is thinner here, and Cassie doesn't look as winded. We run down the remaining stairs and burst outside.

I barely get a breath of fresh air when Tina is on top of me.

She comes at me from behind, smashing me into the ground. I try to scramble up, but she gets on my back and then with a hand pushes the side of my face into the gravel walkway. "You are not getting away with this. And if Val doesn't make it out of that building in the next minute, the rest of your short life will be filled with suffering."

"Enough." I turn in time to see Themis lift Tina in the air as if she weighs no more than a child. "Your brother is coming out right now."

We all turn to watch Val exit the building. Sooty and with burn marks across his chest and arms, he carries someone wrapped in a sheet.

"We need a medic," he yells in a scratchy voice as he falls to his knees. I put her out, but..." He can't say anything more as a coughing fit overtakes him.

Themis takes the sheet-wrapped person from Val, while the released Tina runs to his side.

Peeling the sheet back, she gasps.

"No." A voice from the vamps say. It's Marguerite, the vamp that defended Fern earlier, only to earn Tina's wrath. For her to be this upset...

"Oh no," I say.

"It's Fern." Ms. Themis confirms. She looks out at the

rest of us. "She's still breathing. What was a witch doing in the assassin dorms?"

No one answers, but Marguerite falls to her knees and wails. No one comforts her. I want to go to her but I don't have the right. Fern was nothing but nice to me. She was such a good person. Why did this happen to her?

The medics come and bundle the girl onto a stretcher. One of them also collects Marguerite, who probably will be given some form of magical lithium. Themis watches them go, then turns to Val.

"What happened?"

Tina is on her knees beside her brother. "Can't you see he needs time to recover?"

"It's okay." Val puts a hand on Tina's arm. He coughs and Tina helps him stand. "The alarms went off. Once my door opened and I saw the smoke, I headed toward Tina's room. As I passed the girl's bathroom, I could tell the smoke was coming from there." He glances toward Tina. "I thought it might be..."

She rolls her eyes. "Idiot. I would never get set on fire."

This earns a wry smile from Val. "Well, I decided to check and found Fern. She was on fire, but fighting it. It wasn't a natural fire. She'd cast a spell to put it out and it'd come back again. Like it was determined to burn her alive." Gasps come from all around me.

Themis nods. Grim. "And then?"

"I pushed her into a shower and turned the water up. Then ran to get some sheets and blankets. By the time I came back she was on the ground, smoldering. I wrapped her in the sheet and brought her out here." He coughs again. "That's it."

"You're a hero," Tina says. She looks out at those gathered. By now the whole school has woken up and spilled out of their dorms. She is very clearly working to shape the narrative in real time. As she transfers her gaze to me, I realize I'm part of that narrative as well. "Themis, you of all people know that justice must be served here. We cannot trust this fire breathing unknown shifter living amongst us. We're not safe in our own beds."

"Fern was clearly not in her own bed," Themis replies, dryly.

"That's beside the point," Tina says after only a slight pause. "She was on fire. Who can account for Edie's whereabouts before the fire?"

"I was sleeping," I protest.

"And what about when Jenn died?"

"She was with me," Val disconnects himself from Tina and takes a step toward me. Tina's whole face goes tight and angry.

"No she wasn't."

"Yes, she absolutely was. Earlier today and..." He holds his hand out to me and unsure what else to do, I take it. "And tonight too. We've been secretly seeing each other."

As I gape at him, Val lifts my hand to his lips and lightly kisses my knuckles. It should be a ridiculous gesture, but the cold touch of his lips against my skin burns through me. Meanwhile, there are audible sighs behind me.

Still holding my hand, Val tugs me closer. "There is no way Edie is behind these fires."

And suddenly, he's the one shaping the narrative. The hero of the night, clearing my name. Not just giving me an alibi, but wrapping me up in his own moment.

Themis nods. "All right. Val, get to the infirmary so they can take care of those burns."

Tina steps forward. "I'll go with him."

Val's arm snakes around me. "Actually, Edie will

take me."

Tina's eyes narrow as they focus in on me. There is a new level of ferocity behind her eyes. Before she hated me on principle. But now it's personal.

Val and I make our way through a crowd that parts around us. People seem unsure whether to be awed or scared or impressed. At least until we reach the witch group. Then Val is given endless gentle pats on the back along with soft words of thanks. I glance up at him to see how he's taking this, but he remains as unreadable as ever.

Finally, the crowd fades behind us. For the few feet between us and infirmary, we're alone.

Which gives me limited time to set things straight.

"Um, we're not secretly dating."

"No," he agrees easily. "Not anymore."

Reminding myself that I can't pinch a guy with serious burns, I settle for a sigh. "I mean we're not dating at all."

"You want to break up already?"

"Val." I say his name, exasperated.

"Edie."

We're almost at the infirmary and nowhere close to settling this. I stop. Weirdly, it starts to rain for only the second time since I've been at Mount Olympus. The cool drops fall around us both, and Val groans in pleasure, opening up his burned arms to let them fall on his skin. But I'm not going to be distracted.

"You make no sense. Why didn't you just tell the truth last time and say we were together? Then maybe people would've stopped suspecting me before now and they could've started looking for whoever is really doing this."

Val gives me a long suffering look. "Edie, were things simple where you came from? Or did you just pretend they were, like you're doing now?"

I step away from Val. "If you're gonna be a dick, you can get yourself the rest of the way there." I make it all of three steps before Val is in front of me.

"Okay, wait. You deserve answers." He hesitates, then adds, "some of them, anyway."

"Wow, thanks."

He reaches for me, but I step away. "I didn't say anything the first time because it wouldn't have cleared your name. People think I helped my roommate get away last semester. They don't trust me. My alibi would've made you *less* trustworthy."

"And now because everyone thinks you're a hero the calculus has changed?"

"I guess?" Val holds both hands out and shrugs. "Or at least I hope so."

I cross my arms over my chest, not buying his wide-eyed innocent thing. It's obvious there's ten million more things he's not telling me.

I walk up to Val. His shirt is singed, but I can make out a flamingo and the words, *majestically awkward*. Very purposefully, I poke him in the middle of his chest. "Listen, buddy, I'm not about to get into some fake relationship just because it's convenient." My fingers linger, gently feeling his chest muscles. His t-shirt is soaked now, the solitary rain cloud above us still blessing us with cooling drops.

The corner of Val's mouth lifts ironically. "Oh, I'm fairly certain it will be very inconvenient."

"What's that supposed to mean?" I drop my hand.

"It means that shifters have a way of getting me into trouble and you so far have been nothing *but* trouble."

"Thanks a lot!" I plant my hands on both hips. "I never asked you to help me."

"No, you were just going to stand there and let Tina tear

you apart." Val shakes his head. "I can't let her kill you and have her get kicked out of school."

Realization hits me like a slap. Val doesn't have some secret crush on me. He's just watching out for his sister.

"You know what?" I say. "I think I'll take my chances with Tina."

Spinning on my heel, I walk away. Except I don't make it more than two steps before Val grabs my hand. I try to shake him loose, but for a half burnt dude, he's got a hell of a grip. He forces me around to look at him.

"Don't be stupid, Edie. This goes beyond Tina."

I stop tugging at our linked hands. "What does that mean?"

"The gods are big on revenge."

"Yes, I know. Fire or flood," I say, rolling my eyes. But I'm not even done talking before my tone gets serious instead, as I think about what he just told me—the *gods* are big on revenge. Like he's certain this isn't some petty inter-species student squabble.

"What are you saying?" I ask. "You think one of the teachers is behind this?"

He releases my hand and takes a step back. "I don't know. But I'm saying, be careful who you trust. Students are dying and every one seems fine with all the evidence pointing to you."

I gulp. Hating that he's right. I assumed they were trying to figure out who's behind this...but they don't seem to be trying very hard. "And why should I trust you?" I ask.

Val smiles and puts both hands over his heart. "If you can't trust your fake boyfriend, who can you trust?"

And with that, he marches off, leaving me alone and confused in the darkness, aware that it's stopped raining as suddenly as it began.

24

Darcy meets me halfway to the lagoon, a towel draped over one arm.

I'd told Cassie about my conversation with Themis and how I was on the verge of getting kicked out of the assassination class. She then blabbed it to everyone else. Now the whole school knows. Tina and her friends are, of course, actively rooting against me. But at least my friends are in my corner. It's kinda weird to use that word in the plural, but Greg, Fern, and Darcy—they're all rallying around me, giving advice and basically doing what they can to help me shift.

The only problem is...I haven't mentioned how I might not be ready to shift.

Now Darcy smiles and tosses a towel my way. "Ready for our date?"

"I..." Confused, I give him the side-eye.

A lot of the students at Mount Olympus are pretty casual about sex and dating, but Darcy didn't seem like the kind of guy to make a move on his future date's roommate.

But when I take a better look, I see nothing but humor

in his eyes. Darcy isn't checking me out or being weird, he's just trying to make a joke.

Geez, Greg and his friends really need a new playbook for humor.

"First step is getting into the water," Darcy says as we reach the lagoon. It really is beautiful, but not in a Florida wildlife kind of way. Sure there are mangrove trees, but the water they surround is clear blue. No muddy swamp water here. There's even a waterfall—several merfolk sunbathe on a rock nearby. I avert my eyes from their nudity.

I don't want to be seen as prissy so I just act like it's no biggie. "Yeah, I figured. But what about—" I start to ask, but immediately have to shut up and turn away. Prissy is one thing, but examining your best friend's crush's junk is on a whole other level.

Cassie was not kidding about the merfolk being the least modest species on campus. I hear Darcy's clothes hit the ground, a splash, and then I'm hit by a wall of water.

"Hey!" I push my wet hair out of my eyes to see Darcy smiling, his tail-fin flicking playfully at me just above the surface.

"Get in already!" he says. "The water's fine!"

I strip down to my bathing suit, tossing aside the wet towel. I don't know what the point was of Darcy bringing it for me if he was just going to soak me anyway. Maybe merfolk don't understand the function of a towel in the first place.

I slide into the lagoon and goosebumps roll up my skin, reminding me of the scales from the night of the fire. The water is cooler than any Florida water has the right to be. Apparently, mermen don't understand what "the water's fine" means, either.

I cross my arms in front of me when Darcy swims over,

partly because I'm cold, and partly because the only suit I have is a bikini and I'm distinctly aware of the fact that underneath his school uniform, Cassie's boyfriend is sporting a pretty decent body. Well, the top half, anyway. Right now his bottom half is pretty dolphin-like. No wonder Cassie likes coming to the lagoon with him—his chest is ripped.

"Okay, so we're going to try to relax you a little bit first." Darcy says, circling me. "How are you with floating?"

"I can float" I nod, rolling over onto my back. Darcy's hands support me for a moment, but his touch is cool and light, not staying too long.

I shield my eyes as we float away from the edges and the shade of the trees, the sun beaming down on me. "This reminds me of something Val said," I say, and I feel Darcy tense up beside me.

"He said his old roommate would meditate, and that it helped his whole family with the shifting process."

"Mmm," Darcy says, but doesn't add anything else. I don't know if it's because he doesn't want to talk about Val's werewolf-traitor roommate, or if he doesn't like Val.

"Well, I can't say I know a lot about shifting," Darcy goes on. "We do it automatically in water, but I definitely know about relaxation. Merfolk are very chill." He comes up onto his back beside me, crossing his hands behind his head.

I can't help it. My eyes flick to his crotch...well, his tail area where his crotch would be. He catches me looking and I blush bright red. "Um...sorry"

"It's fine. I'm not shy. Are you wondering about merman anatomy in general or mine in particular? Because I do really like Cassie even if our relationship is taboo."

"I'm not interested in your penis," I shout. The other bathers look over at me and I lower my voice. "I mean, I was just curious. You know, you tell yourself not to look but then you do..."

"Maybe we should get back to working on finding your inner shifter."

"Yes. Gods, please." I say utterly embarrassed.

"First, close your eyes."

I do, and my vision immediately goes red, the sun beating through my eyelids and giving everything the cast of blood. The eyes inside are there in an instant, rolling, searching, almost like they're looking for me.

I gasp and open my eyes, body going taut. I flail, spraying water over both of us as Darcy grabs me.

"Whoa... Okay, yeah, you definitely don't know how to relax."

"Sorry," I say, embarrassed. "Can we try again?"

"Of course." He nods, kicking onto his back easily. "I've got all day."

I take a deep breath, and roll onto my back.

If I want to stay in the assassination class, I need to shift. It was my whole reason for coming here. I'm also not dumb enough to believe that me as plain old Edie Evans will be able to bring down Leviathan. No, I'll have to shift into whatever I am to make that happen.

I just wish I had a little more time to get used to the idea. Like maybe a decade or so...

I force myself to close my eyes. The eyes stare back at me. I force myself to look into them. And think.

Hermes unleashed my wings for me, and I wasn't aware of those brooding, red eyes until I was in the swamps—technically on campus. Maybe being here had woken up something inside of me, weakening Dad's spell that had first started to unwind when I blasted fire during the rogue wave. I'd never been in real danger in my life—Mom and Dad had made sure of that. Like all parents do, of course, but I realize now there was more to it.

They knew that if anything ever truly threatened me, I'd shift without meaning to, protecting myself. That's why they'd always been so careful, making sure I never went too high on the swings, walked home alone at night, or even played any sports, where aggression was encouraged.

I smile a little to myself. They must have been totally thrilled when it turned out I had asthma. Unless...

I almost lose my balance again, but recover, thinking hard. My eyes wide open now. Maybe in more ways than one.

Did my parents *give* me asthma? Did they cast some kind of spell on me that would make for a convenient excuse to not let me out onto a soccer field, where I might accidentally sprout wings or set an opponent on fire? I stopped having breathing problems the second I got on campus—right when I saw the eyes for the first time.

Whatever Dad did, he thought he was protecting me, I remind myself. Of course, they probably didn't know how fast Grandma drove... I wipe a tear away at the thought, then settle my mind back down.

I've got wings, I can make fire, and a few times I've spotted scales forming on my skin. But Merilee and Cassie had laughed at the idea that I might be a dragon, insisting that shifters only changed into regular animals, not mythical ones.

So, what am I?

I make myself relax again, floating back out into the sun, its rays turning everything red again. The eyes are still there, still looking. I know they're looking for me, waiting for me to accept whatever it is that I am. Because whatever they are, is also me, and that's exactly why I'm terrified.

Those eyes shout murder. I shift, sinking under until the water fills my ears, the cold closing over my head and shocking me back into reality—an easier place to be than inside my own head, where red eyes search for me. Eyes that want to kill. Want *me* to kill.

"Okay," I tell Darcy when I surface. "I'm ready to go back."

"Any luck?" he asks, splashing me happily.

"Oh yeah," I tell him, returning a smile. "I feel like I learned something."

Definitely. I learned that I'm a big weenie, too afraid of what's inside of me to ever wanna let it out.

25

The next day in flight class I'm doing everything I can to show Ocypete I'm ready. That's not easy when I'm still rattled by everything that went down last night. At least the news went out this morning that Fern is healing from her burns. Slowly but surely. Themis said by the end of the week she'd be all better and ready to attend the Spring Fling.

Ready to fly; ready for the truth. Unfortunately doing everything I can mostly amounts to getting about five feet off the ground. But it's five more than last week, and I'm sweating when I glide back down to the grass.

"I flew!" I say triumphantly.

"You jumped really high," she corrects me, but she's smiling. Progress is progress. "Now try again. This time once you're in the air I want you to listen to your wings. You can pump all you want, but to fly you've got to find the currents in the air. Your wings will be sensitive to them, if you learn how to interpret what they're trying to tell you."

Listen to my wings? Be one with the air currents? A

couple months ago I would've laughed at this speech. Today, I'm nodding intently.

"Okay," I say, and take a running leap. I spread out my wings, which are a shiny silver at the moment, and try to feel what they're feeling. Instead of thinking about the fact that I have wings—which is what I've been doing—I try to think of them as something separate from me, something with abilities of their own. And desires of their own, too. The wings want to fly. I need to get out of their way.

Sure enough, I feel a downdraft, small and subtle. I turn into it, opening my wings fully. With a whoosh, I'm pulled into the air way faster than I expected, the wings taking full advantage of what I let them do.

"Shit," I say, breathless as I look down at the ground, thirty feet below me.

"You're alright," Ocypete's voice is in my ear as she hovers beside me, her own wings supple and sure. Meanwhile I'm pumping away like a crazy person. "Relax," she says.

I do, and the feeling returns again, each inch of my scaly wings responding to something different in the air. Problem is, my eyes are still on the ground, and I'm completely freaked out.

I plummet. Strong arms encircle my waist at the last moment. Ocypete and I roll together across the grass, me swearing with each bump and her swearing at me.

"You were so close, Edith!" She's yelling at me as she comes to her feet, not with excitement either. "You had it, kid!"

"I know, I just...got frightened." I am embarrassed. And frustrated. This feels like when I kept failing my driving test. Except worse. This is like having a car strapped to my back and being told it's staying there regardless of whether I can figure out how to make it work.

"You're afraid of heights!?" Pity screeches at me. "What kind of flying creature is scared of heights?"

"I'm not scared of heights," I tell her, rubbing my elbow, my wings a crumpled mess around me, and now a dark brown. "I'm scared of falling from them."

Ocypete's wings snap shut behind her and she folds her arms. "Very funny. You're dismissed for the day. Go to the infirmary; that cut above your eye looks pretty nasty."

She turns her back on me and I shout after her, "I think I almost shifted." She pauses. "The night of the fire," I continue. "I...I had scales on my hands."

Her back stiffens so I know she heard me, but she takes flight and I know better than to chase after her; with Pity it's all or nothing. Either I fly and she tells me everything, or I fall and get nothing.

I brush myself off, wiping at a trail of blood coming from above my eye. "Awesome," I say, looking at the red on my fingers. I'm enough of a target for the vamps already, without smelling like dinner.

And one vamp in particular is targeting me. This morning at breakfast, Val showed up and slid onto the bench beside me. Greg went batty—literally—as Val slung an arm around my shoulders and tugged me close.

"So glad we don't have to be secretive anymore, my little wingading," he'd purred as he leaned in for a kiss.

I stuck an elbow in his throat. "It is a relief, my little leech. But remember I told you how much I hate PDA?"

We might've glared at each other for the rest of lunch period, if Cassie hadn't screeched, "Oh wow, you guys make such a cute couple!"

"Screw it," I say under my breath, shaking the memory

of breakfast from my mind, and head for the infirmary. Cassie meets me at the head of the path, holding her wrist.

"What happened?" I ask.

"A baby hydra bit me in Monster Identification," she says, and shows me the two fang marks on the inside of her arm. "What's with your eye?"

"Crash and burn," I say, and immediately regret using the word *burn* when a couple of vamps hiss at me as they walk past. So I guess my fake relationship hasn't cleared my name with the vamps. Here's hoping the healers are feeling more warmly toward me.

"What are you going to do about the dance?" Cassie asks. "Everyone kind of..."

"Hates me?" I can't help but sigh.

I'd been hoping we were done with this subject of conversation. The dance is the last thing on my mind. When I got back to the room last night the first thing she said was, "I can't believe you didn't tell me you were dating Val! Why are you going to the dance with Greg? Is it because of the interspecies taboo?"

I swallowed the urge to tell her the truth. Even Cassie admitted she was not to be trusted with secrets. Instead, I just shrugged and said it was still new and I was afraid Val would dump me and humiliate me in front of the whole school. It was not actually that far from the truth. Then, before Cassie could ask any more questions, I crawled into bed and pulled the covers over my head.

Now she picks right up from last night, her hydra bite not sufficient enough to distract her from the idea of interspecies love. "It's like Twilight. You have to choose between a hot shifter and an even hotter vampire."

"Okay, first of all, how do you know about Twilight?"

"One of the greatest pieces of literature in the modern

age?" Cassie shakes her head in disbelief. "How could I *not* know about it?"

I nod. "Right, of course. But second of all...Greg is not a hot shifter. Most of the time he's Greg and the rest of the time he's a bat. So..."

"Okay, you have a point," Cassie concedes. And I think that's the end of it, but then she turns to me with a look of despair, "So does that mean our double-date is not happening?"

"I don't know," I admit. "I don't know anything."

And to my relief she drops it. For now at least.

26

There's quite a line when we get to the infirmary; apparently Kratos' first year witch class was given weapons before they were ready.

"Hepatitis!" An adult healer yells, straightening from the patient she was leaning over. But the kid's got an open wound in his leg, not a virus. To my surprise, a young woman goes rushing past me, answering the call. She makes some quick notes, nodding all the while.

An orderly rushes past us, knocking into Cassie and not excusing himself as a roll of bandages falls from his hands, leaving a white path on the floor.

"Um, they're like super busy," I say. "Do you want to just—"

But the healer, hands on her hips, pushes us into a room, kicking the door closed behind her.

"What do you need?" she asks brusquely. "You'd better be dying."

"Nice bedside manner," I tell her, and she shrugs.

"You're well enough to stand up. I repeat, what do you need?"

I pull my hand away to show her my cut, and Cassie explains her hydra bite. Hepatitis turns suddenly calm and kind as she looks at our injuries, then angry again when she meets our eyes.

"You'll need waxroot for the hydra bite. I don't have any fresh and don't have time to go cut it." She pulls a small, silver blade from her belt, handing it to Cassie.

"Do you know where the Wall of Weeping is?"

"Yes," Cassie says, eyeing the knife dubiously.

"Waxroot grows there, in between the stones. Go get some, come back and I'll tend to you."

"Hold up," I say, as she's about to turn away. "Is your name really Hepatitis?"

"Yes," she says. "My mother was a healer with a weird sense of humor."

"Um...I was also wondering if we could maybe visit Fern while we're here."

"Fern is in isolation. Her burns are serious and she needs twenty-four seven uninterrupted healing."

"So that's a no, then?"

She crosses her arms and stares me down. "I'm too busy for this shit, and I'm perfectly capable of slipping you some poison rather than healing you, if you keep pushing."

I put both hands in the air, in fake—I think—surrender and Cassie leads me to the Wall of Weeping, which cannot be a great place to hang. Not with a horrible name like that.

As we walk Cassie thankfully chatters about her own love life instead of mine. She still hasn't found a chance to tell Darcy about her prophecy about his death and is debating over exactly when and how to do it. "I was thinking of leaving an anonymous note. That way he won't be mad at me."

"Yeah, but you're the only seer on campus...so he might figure out it's from you," I can't help but point out.

Cassie is disappointed. "Oh, shoot. I didn't think of that. Maybe if I word it just right..." She tugs my arm, leading me toward a more rugged pathway. "The Wall of Weeping is this way."

"Why's it called that?" I ask Cassie, as we head to a different part of campus. This section is older, the foundations of the building giving out a little, the corners not so square. Most of the healing classes are taught on this part of campus, and I realize now that must be because the older buildings harbor plants in their crevices that they harvest. Maybe wild plants are better than the ones they grow in the school greenhouse?

"The Wall of Weeping?" Cassie asks, as she pulls open a door, ushering me inside. The building smells musty, and old.

"It's right next to the Hall of the Dead," she explains. "Used to be there was an enforced mourning period whenever a student died. They'd put their picture up in the Hall of the Dead and make pairs take shifts sitting at a wall in the courtyard, crying and sharing stories of the person who died. It was supposed to be a way to heal some of the rifts between the different students. You know, like make a shifter mourn for vampire, and vice versa. Kind of force everyone to all be on the same team."

"But?" I ask, sensing that there's one coming.

"But a werewolf lost her temper one night while she was supposed to be mourning with a vamp, after another vampire died. She ended up tearing him to pieces."

"Oh," I say. "So they stopped doing it?"

"Yep, nobody really comes here now," Cassie says,

pointing upwards as we enter a long hall. Carved in stone above the entrance it says "Hall of the Dead."

"Super," I say, rubbing my arms for warmth.

"It's alright," Cassie says, taking a torch from the wall. "It's a short hallway. The practice didn't last long."

Still, I'm a little spooked as we enter, the fire from Cassie's torch only reaching a few feet on either side of us. The light bounces off of framed pictures, showing were-wolves in full shifted mode, mermaids with sparkling tails, and vampires looking extremely arrogant and terribly sexy at the same time.

"I mean, why they thought it was a good idea to put a werewolf with a vampire in the first place..." Cassie says.

She stops, her chatter suddenly, eerily silent.

"Cassie?" I ask, and turn to find her staring over my shoulder. I hope she's not about to launch into another death prophecy; I'm not entirely over the one she dropped the other night. But no, her eyes aren't whited out. It's worse—she's staring at something behind me.

"Edie," she says quietly. "I think you should turn around."

I feel heat rising in my chest and it's comforting because it's not fear. I know I can breathe fire right now if I want to. I turn, and the heat is gone, replaced by cold, icy amazement. Staring down at me from the wall is a picture of...me.

"Adrianna Aspostolos," Cassie says, bringing her torch closer to the nameplate under the picture. "Okay, like, not to be rude or anything, but you should be glad your dad took you and you're an Evans. Aspostolos is a mouthful, and I don't even think—"

"Cassie!" I hiss at her. "Could you please...just...be...quiet?"

She does, immediately, and I take a moment to stare at

the picture. She looks exactly like me; blonde hair, darker eyebrows, a little hint of an attitude around the mouth. Then I note the subtle differences. My face is more round, my nose smaller, my chin more delicate.

I take in the photo of the woman who is undoubtedly my mother. Girl, actually. The student in the picture couldn't have been much older than eighteen when she died. Eventually, I start to notice other things—like the fact that her picture frame is clean. I take the torch from Cassie, going from one portrait to the next, confirming my suspicions.

"You were wrong, Cassie," I tell her, handing back the torch. "Someone still comes here, and they're still mourning. Look—her picture has been cleaned recently. All the others have a film of dirt over them."

"What's this?" Cassie leans in closer to the painting, rubs her sleeve across the nameplate to reveal some smaller etchings underneath.

"What's it say?" I ask, leaning in.

"Don't know," Cassie shrugs. "It's in Greek. And that's all Greek to me!"

I don't even pretend to laugh at her joke. Instead I hang the torch in a wall sconce and physically turn Cassie around, digging through her backpack until I find a pen. I hold my arm out and make her painstakingly copy the characters from under Adrianna's portrait onto the inside of my arm.

We're quiet at the Wall of Weeping, Cassie cutting away the waxroot she needs without a word, clutching it in her hands as we pass back through the Hall of the Dead. I try not to look at Adrianna as we pass her, but it's hard not to.

Hepatitis spots us when we return to the infirmary. She immediately chews the waxroot Cassie hands her and presses it against her hydra bites, instructing her to keep the pressure steady.

"Now you," she says, and I hold my hair out of my eyes so she can see the cut on my forehead.

"What is this?" she snaps, grabbing my wrist.

"I got hurt flying—"

"No"—she squeezes my wrist tighter, grinding my bones — "this!" She stabs a finger at the writing on my arm.

"Can you read it?" I ask her.

"Of course I can read it," she says. "All healers are trained in Greek. Wait—do you not know what this says?"

"No," Cassie and I eye each other as Hepatitis pours some water onto the edge of her apron and starts rubbing out the letters.

"Hey!" I jerk back. "I need to know what that says."

She grabs my arm and pulls it against her again, trapping my elbow in her armpit while she wipes the pen marks away.

"You can't let anyone see it," she says, rubbing so hard that it hurts. "Students used to think that just writing words like this onto someone's skin could be used as a curse. Like if you write it, it will come true. I don't think it actually works, but we don't want people getting ideas, the way things are going right now."

"No," I agree, pulling my arm back and wincing when I see how raw and red it is. "Now, tell me. What did that say?"

Hepatitis looks around her, and lowers her voice. "It said, *died in childbirth*."

27

I flee the infirmary, leaving Cassie behind, determined to go straight back to the Wall of Weeping and search some more. Unfortunately, I run smack into Greg. Like, literally.

"Hey, Edie," he stares at my face. "Did I do that?"

"What?" I reach up and touch my cut. I forgot to get it healed. "No, I crashed in flying class. Wait..." I search my bag and find the magic spray I swiped the first time I was injured.

"I can help you," Greg offers and takes the can from me. He studies the wound and sprays it gently. It stings at first, then takes away the pain. I wish I could spray it on my life.

Greg hands me back the can. "So you and Val, huh?"

"It's complicated," I tell him. "But you and I were only ever going to the dance as friends—you know that, right?"

He looks hurt but it's important he knows. "Yeah, sure, of course. Friends with an option to procreate."

I shake my head and he offers a small smile, one that makes me think maybe all of his mating jokes might actually be his horrible attempt at humor. I manage to smile back.

"But we're still going together, right?" he asks. "You're not going to ditch me, are you?"

"I wouldn't do that to a friend," I assure him.

"Where are you off to now?" he asks.

"I was going to..." What? Try to find answers that never seem to come? Stare at the picture of my dead mother? Try not to run into any blood thirsty vamps? If only Ocypete would give me the answers I need.

An idea hits me like a bolt of action. "Greg, can you shift like me?"

"Uh..." His stricken look clearly says he doesn't think of what I do as shifting.

"Can you pop out just your wings?" I clarify.

"Yes, since I was like, two," he huffs.

"And if you're in human form they're..." I don't know how to be kind about it. "Regular size?"

"Yes," he says, stiffening a bit. "I'm big where it counts."

I'm beyond caring if he thinks I'm making dick jokes. "I need you to give me a ride."

He raises his eyebrows.

"Not a sex ride. A flying ride...like a winged Uber!"

"A ride to where?

"Ocypete's nest."

"Oh hells no." He shakes his head. "Not happening. She is super scary."

"I just need you to get me there. You don't have to stay." In fact, I really don't want him to. "Please?"

I try to turn on the charm. I am a horrible person. After relegating him to the friend zone I'm using my wiles to convince him to help me. But awful or not, it's working.

"I guess."

I jump toward him and grab his hand. "Great! Let's go."

"Now?"

"No time like the present." I look him up and down. He's fit but not like the vamps. More in a sinewy kind of way. "Are you going to be able to carry me?"

"Oh ye of little faith." He sweeps me up in his arms and his large black wings unfurl around him. I have to admit that the dip in my stomach isn't entirely because of the sudden ascent. Greg is surprisingly strong, and there's a confidence to him in the air that he doesn't have on the ground.

I try not to look down as we fly over the school, pass into the swamp and head toward the biggest Cyprus tree I have ever seen in my life. Greg circles twice, and I know he's checking for Pity before he sets me on the edge of her "nest."

It's more like a treehouse, with molted feathers and mud filling in the cracks, but I can see well-worn perching spots on a branch outside the door where my flying instructor must spend most of her time—her equivalent of the front porch rocking chair. The deep claw marks are unmistakable.

"You alright?" Greg asks, putting me down on the large branch. I turn back to him, suddenly grateful for this weird little guy.

"Yes, thank you." I give him a hug, safely friend-zoning him by not adding a squeeze or letting our chests touch. He takes the hug—and the hint—before he soars off, and there's a little bit of envy in it as I watch him go, wings spread fully as he heads back to the school. There's a familiar tickle in my back, and I give in to the pressure that had been begging to release while we were in the air. My wings stretch out behind me, brightly magenta today.

Ocypete is nowhere in sight, but I'm not tempted to

snoop. I might not have had enough lessons to know how to fly, but I learned quickly enough how silently she can swoop through the air, and how sharp her talons are. No, whatever secrets Ocypete has, I'll need to come by them honestly. Well, somewhat honestly. 'Cause I am totally lying about how I got here.

I've wandered out as far as I dare go, only treading on the thickest parts of a branch and barely screwing up the courage to glance at the ground—easily a hundred feet below—when there's a slight sway under my feet, and Ocypete is behind me. My wings automatically adjust, like a tightrope walker's bar, and I keep my balance with surprising ease.

"Well," Ocypete says, eyeing me. "Look what the cat dragged in. Sorry," she says, spotting my confusion. "That's an old harpy joke. I shouldn't have taught it to you. Don't ever say it to another harpy, or you'll be in for it."

"Another harpy...like my grandma?" I ask.

"Ah," Ocypete raises her head an inch higher, looking down her nose at me. "Yes," she admits.

"My grandma who isn't actually my grandma by blood?" I push.

"Perhaps we should sit," Pity says, folding her wings away and gesturing me to do the same. We go into her house, which is full of wicker furniture. I settle myself into a chair, only to have her hop onto the arm, her talons dangerously close to my leg.

"What do you know?" she asks, as if resigning herself to filling in the blanks.

"I know that my parents are not who I thought they were," I tell her. "They adopted me. Took me and my sister from here. I know that my biological mother was Adrianna Apos—"

"Blah, blah, blah," Ocypete says, unfurling her wings in irritation and gliding over to a couch, where she neglects the cushions to perch on the back. "What do you know that actually *matters*?"

"Excuse me?" I sputter, and she rolls her eyes. "My entire life being a lie doesn't *matter*?"

"Oh, you thought it was all about *you*, right? Thought I was going to reveal that you were some amazing key to a magical puzzle, a spectacular gift that we've been searching for since you left?"

"I..." Okay, well yeah, maybe I was thinking something like that. "Val did say—"

"Val?" Pity's thin eyebrows go up halfway to her hairline —and that's receding so her surprise is palpable. "A little interspecies love in your future?"

"My past, maybe," I mutter to myself, embarrassed all over again that I actually thought Val really liked me.

"What did Val say?" Ocypete prompts me to continue.

"Not long after I got to the school, after he saw my wings he said, '*No wonder they were looking for you*'."

"Hmmpphh." She nuzzles in her armpit for a second, idly spitting out a stray feather. I've been around shifters enough by now to realize that sudden grooming is usually a sign of stress.

"They *were* looking for me? And who are *they* anyway?"

"The gods," she admits. "You're a pawn being used to play a game much more dangerous than you can ever imagine. Who your mother was, who your father is, that's all inconsequential."

My face burns. Inconsequential? What could be more important to me than that? I lean forward. "You told me if I made it to your nest, I'd be ready for the truth. I'm here—so tell me."

"Alright, little girl." Ocypete lets out a cackle. "You think you're ready, that you're a hero, ready to avenge the deaths of the people you love, isn't that so?"

I nod solemnly, fingernails cutting into my palms as I make fists. Ocypete's head bobs as she talks, warming to her speech.

"And what side do heroes fight on?" she asks.

"The side of right," I tell her, conviction in my voice.

She hops from the back of the couch to the cushion, her talons making skittering noises as she moves onto another chair, eyes fastened on mine as she comes closer, her voice almost a whisper now.

"But what if you're wrong about who is right?"

I'm out of my chair in a moment, hands still in fists, anger making my voice wobble. "I'm not wrong. Monsters killed my father!"

"They killed a man who *posed* as your father," Pity corrects me. "And why do you suppose they did that? Who was your adoptive father trying to protect you from?"

I think of the panicked voicemail on Dad's phone, Mom's voice saying, *they're here*, the face of Leviathan as he swept over my father.

"Levi," I tell her. "And his kind."

"His kind? You know, I'm technically a monster..."

"But you're different!"

"Am I? I'm tolerated here because I serve. But I'm not treated as an equal to the gods."

"You're saying that Dad wasn't trying to protect me from the monsters?" I don't bother to hide my skepticism.

Ocypete nods as if she's agreeing with me, but then her brow furrows in fake concentration. "Then why would he take you away from a school where entire armies are trained to fight monsters? Wouldn't that be the safest place on earth for you?"

"I... I..." My hands are unclenching, my conviction faltering.

She wobbles closer. Her mouth is only inches from my ear when she asks, "Why would he run *away* from the gods?"

"And why would he send me *back*?" I yell at her, latching onto the thought. "The password was one of the last things he said to me. He said I should go with—"

"Ichor," Ocypete says calmly. "The password was ichor. Your father wanted you to come with me, not Hermes. Unfortunately, he found you first, and brought you here. Right where the gods want you."

I slump, all of my conviction gone.

Ocypete moves closer to me, suddenly quiet and cautious. "What are you thinking, child?"

"I don't know," I suddenly scream, all my frustration escaping me as my wings unfurl, darkly scarlet with rage. "I don't know anything," I yell at her, tears rolling down my cheeks. "I don't know who to trust or what's going on here, I just... I just..." I stop, choking on a sob. I'd been about to say, *I just want to go home.*

But I don't have one of those. Not anymore.

28

Ocypete takes pity on me and makes me a cup of tea, gently asking me to put my wings away when I accidentally break a Precious Moments she had resting on the coffee table. I take the tea, apologize for the figurine, and lean back in my chair.

"So...you're telling me the gods are bad?" I ask.

Pity nods, her head moving rapidly up and down in the way that all the bird-shifters have. "Of course they would say the monsters are bad. War is a matter of perspective, dear."

"I really don't need a philosophy lesson," I tell her, spitting out a mouthful of too-hot tea.

"Alright, then how about some history?" she asks, and I nod.

"Many of the monsters were made for the sport of the gods—some of them as a direct result of the gods at their own sport. You know about the Minotaur, right?"

I shudder a little. That story had made me a little ill when they taught it in history class. The nymph Pasiphaë—the daughter of a god—had been as sexually fluid as Hermes, and thought some fun with a bull might make her happy. Whether or not she had any fun, she did get a kid out of it—the Minotaur. Except we also learned that she loved her misbegotten child. He was the one who turned on her.

"And Scylla?" Pity asks.

"Uh..." I wrack my brain, but can't come up with anything.

"Circe—another nymph, the daughter of a god, and a powerful witch as well—she envied Scylla her beauty."

I shake my head. "Wait, no, I checked out a book from the library called The History of Monsters. Scylla was a horribly ugly, awful monster. She hates Circe. And all witches, too."

"No," the harpy shakes her head. "Scylla was a beauty, loved by many—and by a man that Circe wanted for herself. So she turned her rival into the monster we know today. Very few people remember what Scylla was...only what she's become."

Ocypete hops to a windowsill and perches, watching the sun as it starts to sink. "I could go on. There are many monsters, Edie. Most of them owe their creation to the gods either as playthings or pets, bastards or by-blows, all discarded once they ceased to be interesting. This war has been going on for centuries, with the gods not even fighting their own battles. No." She shakes her head, and turns back to me. "Why would they? They get *you* to do it for them."

"A pawn." I repeat her words from earlier. "You think we're all just being trained to fight for the gods, because they can't be bothered to fight for themselves?"

"Oh, they could be bothered," she says. "That's part of what makes it so infuriating. They can't die; they're immortal. But they're also a bunch of gods-damned dick weeds."

I spit out my tea again, this time in shock. Hearing that

kind of language from Pity is sort of like hearing it from my grandma—somehow fitting, and absolutely hilarious.

"Honestly," she insists. "They can't stand to get hurt. Even the smallest little trifle and they go hide in caves, and cry, and act like someone lopped their whole arm off. When you spend an immortal life free of pain, even the smallest amount is terrifying."

I nod, thinking. "So, the gods are using us like...human shields?"

She wiggles one clawed hand in the air. "Sort of human shields. Paranormal shields."

"And you're telling me because..." I let my words trail off, watching her face for a clues, when it hits me—hard.

"Oh my gods." I'm on my feet in a second, tea spilling everywhere. "You're working for them, aren't you? You're... you're..."

"A spy." She nods, and takes a prim sip of tea. "And I'd like for you to be one, too."

My foot slips in spilled tea, and I hit the floor in a flash of plaid skirt, my wings popping out—now an alarmed yellow—knocking over a lamp.

"Maybe not a very good spy," she says, eyeing me over the edge of her cup. "Based on that display."

"I...you..." I'm shaking, my butt is soaked in tea, and there's hardly any light left in Ocypete's house now that the sun is setting and I broke the only lamp.

"You need to think about it a little," she says, leaning forward and resting her tea on the slightly skewed coffee table. "I understand."

"I need to think a lot," I correct. "You just dropped a bomb on me. I don't know if I believe you."

"Of course," she agrees, rising to help me to my feet.

"Which is why I'm not going to pressure you. But, Edie, you realize I must ask you to keep all this to yourself?"

"Right," I nod, as she guides me to the door, stopping only when another thought occurs to me. "Wait—you didn't kill Jenn, did you? Or the one bat boy? Or burn Fern, or—"

"Those were all mine," she says quickly, an edge to her voice.

"Yours!" I jerk my arm from her grasp.

"Mine," she says again, quietly this time, with a hint of affection. "They were my spies."

"Oh," I say.

"So you see, Edie," she goes on, leading me to the edge of her platform. "I don't have to threaten you at all to keep you from going to the gods with news of my treachery. You're in danger just by knowing."

And with that, she pushes me off the edge.

29

She's trying to kill me, I think as my wings flair out, desperately trying to keep me airborne even as I crash through the tree branches.

She told me too much. She doesn't trust me.

Thoughts are tumbling through my head as I spin, and the ground is coming at me alarmingly fast when I realize the truth—Ocypete thought I'd mastered flying.

That was our deal; I fly to her place, she comes clean. She fulfilled her end of the bargain, it's my own fault that I'm going to die in a pile of broken legs, arms...and wings.

Wings, dammit. I have wings. So...use them.

I pump, spread them wider, do everything that has failed me on the practice fields, to no avail. And then, right when I'm about to come to an alarmingly final stop, I feel those eyes again, red, heavy...terrifying. Whatever belongs to those eyes has wings, too. And so do I. Time to embrace that —or at least, the part that I need the most right now.

I take a deep breath...and give up.

I've got the space of half a second to stop being Edie, the teenager from Florida, and start being whatever I actually am. And amazingly, it works. The moment I let go of everything I think of as me—everything that is human—my wings take control.

Almost too quickly.

I'm thrust upward, branches I managed to avoid on the way down getting their smacks in as I ascend. But I'm laughing, the lift in my stomach spreading to my face as a smile cracks.

I'm flying, dammit. Despite everything that's messed up in my life, this is amazing. I turn and soar over the trees, literally above it all.

I sweep in toward the ground and realize that while I may have figured out how to fly, I certainly have not figured out how to land. I crash awkwardly into the soil, actually rolling head over heels. But the ground is wet and springy, and I'm too happy to care that I'm covered in dirt.

I stand and brush myself off. My legs are scraped to hell, but this time I remember the magic spray I keep in my bag and I'm fixed up in no time. My uniform is fine...not even a tear. I should expect nothing less from shape changing magic cloth.

After I sort myself out I head back toward the school. Everything Ocypete told me fits, but I don't want to believe her. The gods are responsible for the war? For the student's deaths? Even for my father's murder?

I know Ocypete believes it's all true, but that doesn't mean that it is. I can't forget what Merilee said about how dementia isn't exclusive only to humans. Pity might have actually cracked. I detour back to the Weeping Wall, scrambling through the ruins and finding my mother's photo. I stare at it for a while, wondering what my life would have been like if she lived. Who would I have been? Who is my father?

"She was one of our best students," a voice says from behind me and I turn to find Themis. Her perfect neatness is out of place in these ruins.

"You knew...she was my mother?" I ask. Though it's not really a question.

"Yes."

"And you didn't tell me?" I spit out the words, full of venom.

"I wanted to protect you. I wanted to protect your father..."

"Well you did a bang up job. My bio mom is dead. My adoptive dad is dead. Who knows where the rest of my family is? And I'm stuck here, not knowing who to trust."

A noise escapes Themis' mouth and it takes me a moment to realize she is sobbing. I want to stay angry but her emotion is so raw...I go to her side.

She puts her hand on my shoulder and sinks to the ground, taking me with her. "I loved your father. I loved him like he was my own son."

"You raised him." I prompt. Tears are filling my own eyes at the thought of him and I swallow the knot in my throat.

"He was a foundling. He just appeared in the marsh. A gift...I fought to keep him. The second I saw him, I knew he was meant to be my son."

I hadn't realized how much Themis loved him. I hadn't thought about what his death must have done to her. "Tell me about him," I say.

Themis wipes her tears, her face impossibly perfect. "He was smart and so good. He always stood up for anyone who was picked on. He didn't think it was right that the girls who got pregnant were kicked out. He begged me to do something, so I did. First with Mavis's mom. She motions to another photograph with the name Bella Demopoulous written under it. Like my mother's, it's been kept clean all these years.

"Then with yours," she says, pointing to Adrianna Aspostolos. "A spell was cast to hide their condition. But it didn't matter in the end."

"It was you," I said, looking between the two portraits. "You were the one who took care of their pictures."

"Yes, it was the least they deserved, dying the way they did." Themis shudders at the thought. "I took you both in. But as Mavis grew it was harder and harder to hide both of you on campus. She was always in to everything.

"Your father...he knew it was only a matter of time. He and your mother were together then and agreed to take you away from here. The day they left was the hardest of my life. Watching three of my children—that's how I thought of you all—disappear. But I knew it was for the best. If you were found you would have been destroyed."

"*Destroyed*? Why?"

She chokes off a sob, gets to her feet and looks down at me. "I've told you too much, but I hope you understand now why we all did the things we did. Whisking you away, the spells to keep you hidden and to stop you from shifting..."

"If you did all that, then please do one last thing and let me stay in the assassination class. I figured out flying today and I'm sure shifting will happen soon. If I could just have a little more time—"

Themis is already shaking her head. "No, Edie. I'm sorry. The deadline is firm. It's not my decision alone."

I nod, thinking of how I'd embraced my wings and finally been able to fly. How will I ever get past my fear of those red eyes, and the fire within them? How can I ever equate *that* with *me*?

"If I shift before the dance this weekend, though, I stay,

right?"

"That was the bargain. I will make sure the Academy honors it." Themis turns to leave, but I reach out, stopping just short of actually touching her.

"Wait, do you know what I am?" I ask. "I...the night of the fire...my hands had scales..."

"Scales? I truly don't know what you might be. But I have a feeling it will be spectacular." She gives my cheek one last caress. "Please," she tells me. "Try to stay out of trouble."

I scramble to my feet. "Thank you. For everything you did for me. For everything you did for my father."

She nods tightly and I decide to push my luck. "Look, I heard some rumors that the gods aren't everything they seem. That they're just using us in the war against the monsters..."

The slap comes out of nowhere and for a moment I can barely believe it's happened. Then my face burns and I stare at Themis with wide, hurt eyes.

"Don't you ever say anything like that again. Don't even think it," she tells me. But it's not anger I hear in her voice—it's fear. She pulls me in for a tight hug, then pushes me away just as forcefully and flees the ruins.

"Wait!" I yell after her. But she's gone.

So many emotions are swirling around in me. I once again stare at the mother I never had a chance to know. I go to Bella's portrait as well, to study it. Mavis' similarities with her birth mother are not as strong as mine are with mine, but there's a resemblance. Bella Demopoulos has the same inscription under her portrait as my mother—*died in childbirth*.

I touch it gently. I have so many questions still, but one stands out.

Who is my father?

30

I have more important things to do than get ready for a dance. I don't know who my father is. I've never properly mourned my mother. I'm suspected of setting fire to my classmates, and am more than likely a pawn in a war pitting gods against monsters.

But what am I doing?

I'm worried about clothes and makeup because it's the day of the Spring Fling.

Val continues to play my fake suitor. It has helped make things a little less tense around campus. After saving Fern, Val is a hero. Having him vouch for me—and Fern backing him up—has taken away most of the suspicion. Even better, Tina has refrained from murdering me. Sure, she looks at me like she's imagining my death, but doesn't say a word. Val must have spoken with her.

In the meantime, I've gotten used to Val at my side all the time. Every day we cycle through multiple awful pet names for each other. I've started studying a thesaurus at night just to give myself options for the next day.

Overall, as far as fake boyfriends go Val isn't too bad.

Actually, he's pretty great. The worst part is reminding myself it's fake. Every day, though, it's more difficult. I'm afraid I'm starting to fall for him.

I'm actually grateful for the stupid double date. If I was going with Val we'd end up slow dancing—probably more than once—and I don't think my little heart could take it. Right now my plan is to stick to Greg like a burr.

Unfortunately, Val seems to have forgotten what I told him ages ago—that I'm going to the Spring Fling with Greg. I realize this when he slides into his now usual seat beside me at lunch and asks, "So what time should I pick you up tonight, my little pigeon?"

I sigh. He's been on a bird name thing lately.

Greg isn't amused either. He's gotten in the habit of sitting across from me so he can be better positioned to glare at Val. "Excuse me, Val. But tonight Edie is *my* little pigeon."

I generally try to ignore Greg and Val when they get into these little cockfights, but I have to straighten one thing out before this goes any further.

"I'm not anyone's little pigeon. And you knew about this, Val. I told you that day in Kratos' class."

Val looks from me to Greg and then back to me. I could almost swear he looks a little bit hurt, but then he smirks. "That's right. The pity date."

Greg's whole face falls. "I should go. Wanted to be early for class, talk to the teacher—you know."

He stands and grabs his full tray at the same time. An apple rolls off and Val catches it with one hand and then takes a big noisy bite.

"Greg, wait," I say, but he's already gone.

"They cancelled afternoon classes so we could get ready

for the dance," Cassie, who witnessed this whole thing, finally pipes up.

"Maybe he forgot," Val drawls, looking not the slightest bit contrite. "You know, he can be a little...*batty*."

I smack the apple out of his hand. "Why are you being such a dick?"

"Oh c'mon," Val picks the apple off the table and takes another bite. It's the first time I've ever seen him eat anything and it's a little bit distracting. The way his teeth slice through the apple—it's like watching one of those infomercials for a super sharp knife. "It's not like you actually *want* to go with Greg."

"Yeah, well did you ever think that maybe I don't want to go with you either?"

"Oh?" Val's eyebrows raise and again I almost imagine hurt there, but then he smiles. "You're right. I didn't realize. I thought...well, I assumed I was the only one bored with this relationship. It seemed churlish to break up with you when you're already at such a low point. The shifter who can't shift. With only days left in the assassination class. I had planned... well, never mind that now. It's much better this way. A clean break on both sides. Ending it before it gets ugly."

He brushes his lips against my cheek. A there and then gone kiss with a cold that lingers. "Good-bye little chickadee. It's been fun." He stands and leaves with all the grace that Greg lacked.

I watch him go, unsure of what just happened.

Apparently, I'm not the only one. Cassie leans across the table and whispers, "Was that a fake breakup or a real one?"

"Real thing, I think." I swallow, my throat tight. For a fake boyfriend, that felt like a very real dumping.

Cassie stands and holds out a hand. "C'mon, let's go up

to the room so you have time to cry and then put a cold washcloth on your face afterwards so you're not all puffy for the dance. And I've got some great concealer you can try out because, trust me, I cried a lot before you showed up."

"I'm not going to cry," I protest, but I take her hand and let her lead me out of the cafeteria. Around us everyone is chattering with excitement about the dance and I just want to get away from them all. Throwing open the door, I walk straight into Darcy. Our heads knock together and we both stumble back.

"Oh no, are you okay?" Cassie rushes over to Darcy while I blink and see stars.

"I'm fine." Darcy jerks his chin in my direction. "Sorry, Edie. I wasn't watching where I was going." He laughs, but the sound is strained. "It's been a weird day. Someone sent me this threatening note. I took it to Themis and she thought it was just a prank. But I don't know."

"Threatening note?" Cassie says in an odd high-pitched voice.

Darcy pats her arm. "It's okay. Themis is probably right. Just someone's idea of a bad joke."

Cassie gulps. "Can I see it?"

Darcy hesitates and then shrugs. "Sure." He digs into his pocket and pulls out a creased piece of paper.

Cassie quickly reads it and says, "Oh." She passes it over to me.

Watch your step at the dance tonight. You're the next to die.

"It might not be a threat. That could read like a warning, or a pre—" I stop short, realizing with a horrible blinding clarity who must have sent that note. I glance at Cassie who grimaces back at me, confirming my suspicion.

Apparently, she finally decided to tell Darcy about her vision. And in the worst way possible.

"Well, we'll definitely have your back tonight," I reassure him.

"Yeah. Totes. Def," Cassie echoes my sentiment. We make plans to meet outside of the grand hall where the dance will be held, before heading in opposite directions.

As we walk away, I look at Cassie and she shrugs sheepishly. "I probably could've worded that a little bit better, huh?"

"You think?" Despite my fight with Val I laugh. "Well, at least Darcy will be on his toes tonight."

"We won't let anything happen to him, right?" Cassie asks in a scared voice.

I squeeze her hand. "Of course we won't!"

There's no more putting it off—it's time to get ready for the dance.

"So we just wear our uniforms?" I ask.

"Yeah." There's a light knock on the door. Cassie screeches and runs to it and I am absolutely confused until she opens it to reveal a fully healed Fern.

"Oh my gods, Fern!" I yell. "I'm so glad you're okay." She looks good as new. No burns. No scars. "We tried to visit you but we weren't allowed."

"No one was," she tells me, stepping into the room. "Cassie invited me to get ready with you guys, hope that's okay."

"Of course it is! But don't you have a witch crew you're a part of?" I realize at once it's the wrong thing to say.

"They're not really talking to me right now."

"What, you almost died! Why are they mad?"

"Well, it came out that I was with Marguerite and..."

"They're upset you're a lesbian?" I ask.

"Nothing so pre-historic. They're upset I'm with a vampire."

"Oh." I guess I'm lucky all my friends are really accepting of inter-species relationships.

"Well, we don't care who you date," Cassie assures her.

"Yeah, Cassie is in love with a fish," I add, teasing.

Cassie laughs. "Whatever. At least I'm not in the bloodsucker fan club."

Fern and I exchange a glance. "So you and Val are an official thing now?"

"We were. Kind of." I throw up my hands. "He broke up with me at lunch. I think. It's super complicated."

"Dating a vampire always is. Marguerite was so cool in public, but when we're alone—

she's fire. I haven't spoken to her since the accident. I hope she realizes that I'm not lying about..." She pauses and it gets quiet for a minute. We'd all heard the rumor that Fern knew nothing about who her attacker was, even when a healer tried all of their restorative memory charms on her. I hope it wasn't Hepatitis who tried, for Fern's sake.

"You still can't remember?" I ask, but Fern shakes her head.

"Okay, gods, let's change the subject." Cassie butts in. "It's time to get ready."

I look around. "Aren't we suppose to wear our uniforms? Aren't we already all ready?"

Fern and Cassie look at each other, then burst out laughing.

"I'll go first," Fern says and she closes her eyes, her lip twitching. When she opens them she is no longer wearing her uniform but a beautiful flowing ball gown. It's silver and sparkly and suits her lithe figure perfectly.

"No. Freaking. Way." Our uniforms can change? Why did no one tell me this?

"It's only for tonight," Cassie answers my unasked question. "They tweak the spell for dances. The idea is that your uniform can change into what represents you best, whatever you are—or whatever you most want to be—deep down. Look, I'll go next."

She closes her eyes and when she opens them she's in an aqua blue mermaid tail cut gown. It's beaded to look like scales.

I bark out a laugh. "Really playing up the merfolk angle," I tell her.

"Is it too much?" she asks.

"No! You look awesome. I should have said that first."

She grins. "Okay, now you. Close your eyes and think about how you want to look...or how you want to feel."

I close my eyes and try not to think of Val, but that's where my mind goes. Why is he such a dick!? I shake my head. I don't want to impress him. I want to look amazing for myself. I want to...I open my eyes.

Fern and Cassie gasp and I look in the mirror. My dress is blood red. It's low cut, sleeveless and hugs my body. A slit in the side shows off my long legs.

"Damn, girl." Cassie whistles.

"It's okay?" I ask.

"If I wasn't a taken woman..." Fern jokes.

"Okay, okay," I say, embarrassed. "Let's go meet our dates."

Dressed to kill, we head to the dance.

31

I'm doubtful when Cassie leads us to the dining hall. How lame is throwing a dance in the cafeteria? But when we enter, it looks like a completely different place. Bigger, with cathedral ceilings, a dance floor, and a live band playing modern music. I stop, shocked. It's just like any other school dance except fancier and with better looking people.

The staff is there too, and Kratos is—somehow—even more attractive with a shirt *on*. Hermes is bouncing from group to group, not knowing who to flirt with. The only person he doesn't even try anything with is Themis, who is standing by herself in a corner, devastatingly gorgeous in a little black dress and killer heels. But her manner is anything but approachable; she's got her wine glass in a grip that's going to shatter it if she's not careful, and her face is made of stone. I can't believe this is the same woman who hugged me at the Wall of Weeping. She's tense as hell, every line of her body ready to react to danger.

A burst of laughter grabs my attention and a tall, beautiful redhead with flowers in her hair separates from Kratos, her eyes sweeping the students. Several girls step in front of their boyfriends, and more than a few of the boys are happy to cower behind their dates, although one or two return her glances.

"Persephone," Cassie whispers to me. "Keep a close eye on Val, or you might lose him."

"I'm here with Greg," I say, stiffly.

"Ha," Cassie laughs. "Persephone has a type, and Greg is not it. He's safe from being a boy toy."

As if we'd conjured him with a word, Greg appears out of nowhere, towing Darcy with him.

"You look...just...wow," Greg tells me.

"You have such a way with words," I say, but I blush. Greg's actually cute in a tux and bowtie. Little stitched bats dot his cummerbund. Darcy is wearing a deep blue that complements Cassie's dress perfectly.

"Let's dance!" Fern says, making her way onto the dance floor, not caring that she doesn't have a partner. We follow and soon my slight feelings of embarrassment leave me. We're having fun!

Fern isn't dancing by herself for long. Marguerite appears at her side. She's wearing a beautiful A-line sparkly gold dress. She and Fern are silver and gold. Fern stops dancing and I wonder which way it will go. A loving reunion or a quarrel on the dance floor.

Marguerite holds out her hands and Fern takes them with a smile. In an instant they are in each other's arms, and Marguerite whispers something into her ear.

"Awww," Greg says.

"Yeah, super aww. But Tina looks pissed," I tell him. Just past the girls she glowers, running her mouth to her vampire friends. "I think Marguerite is on the outs with the popular kids."

"She can always join our crew," Greg says.

"Do we have a crew?" I ask.

"Sure! We're the lovable losers."

"Hey! Speak for yourself." I swat at his arm.

"I am," he says, awkwardly confident, as usual. "I'm lovable."

"And maybe not quite such a loser," I admit.

The music changes to a slow dance and Greg gets a dreamy look in his eyes. Oh no, I picked the wrong time to drop a compliment. He comes in for the close contact slow dance, and I'm wondering how I'm going to do the one-millionth friendly-fend-off with him, when suddenly Val is in between us. He's wearing one of those cheesy tuxedo t-shirts. Yet somehow, on him, it doesn't look cheesy at all.

"Can I have this dance?' he asks.

"I thought you broke up!" Greg's head pops around Val.

Val sweeps me in his arms and away before Greg can finish his sentence, which is incredibly rude to my date, but then Val is holding me against him and I don't even care.

"You look like a vampire in that dress," Val tells me.

I can't help but laugh. "Why do I get the feeling that's meant to be the biggest compliment you could ever give me?"

"It is." He pulls me in closer.

I remind myself not to melt into a big gooey puddle. "So good news. Everyone heard about our break up and no one has tried to kill me. So I think it's safe for us to stop fake dating."

Val spins me and the room whirls by in a colorful blur. "What if I don't want to?"

"Um, you broke up with me," I remind him.

He smiles faintly. "Everyone says that shifters are territorial, but the truth is that vampires are way worse."

"Yeah," I nod. "I've heard the tracker dorms stink because the werewolves pee on everything."

Val laughs. "I've heard that too." He dips me. "But that's not quite what I meant."

"No, I get it. You were jealous of Greg."

"Jealous of Greg? No." Val makes a face like this is absurd. "I just got the sense that you weren't into this whole relationship."

"Fake relationship," I remind him.

"Fake relationship for your benefit," he adds.

"I thought it was for Tina's. So she didn't get expelled for killing me?"

Val rolls his eyes. "She wouldn't have touched you. I was worried about you, okay? You're so...helpless."

"Helpless?" I push away. "I'm the girl who set you on fire, remember?"

"Why are you mad?" Val shakes his head. "Tensions were high. They still are. I offered you my protection."

I put my hands on my hips.

Suddenly we are no longer dancing. We are standing in the middle of the dance floor, arguing.

"Why?" I ask, suddenly wanting all the cards on the table. "Why help me? You barely know me. Why were you so concerned that you were willing to put yourself out?"

Val stares at me with that unreadable expression. Then he sighs. "Do you want to hear that I'm attracted to you, Edie? Will that make you feel better? You want me falling at your feet like Greg does?"

It is so condescending and...I don't even know what. My palm itches to slap the smug expression off his face.

"Excuse me," Persephone is suddenly beside us and then with another blink she's attached herself to Val like a curvy redheaded leech. "Mind if I cut in here?"

"Darcy, please just listen!" I hear someone wail from the other end of the dance floor. It seems like Val and I aren't the only ones not having a great time.

I glance around and spot Cassie and Darcy arguing loudly.

"Actually, we're still dancing," Val says, reaching for me. I glance back at Cassie and Darcy in time to see him storm off.

"Actually," I say, "This is perfect timing. Enjoy your dance."

Persephone smiles and loops both arms around Val's neck. After a moment Val settles his hands around her hips. A little lower than necessary, if you ask me. He raises an eyebrow at me over Persephone's shoulder, before turning his attention to her with one of his slanted smiles.

I am torn between jealousy and hoping she drains all the smug out of him, even if she does it through his...I shake my head. Okay, no, actually that image does bother me. I hurry away to Cassie, who is in tears.

"What happened?" I ask.

"I told him it was me who sent the note. I tried to explain but he thought it was a prank. He was really mad. He said Themis was super upset about the whole thing, and said she'd be making sure the staff was extra vigilant tonight. So they're all on edge because of me, and I... I..."

"It's okay," I tell her. "Let's go after him. I'll help you explain."

"Oh, thank you!" She grabs my hand and pulls me off the dance floor. We head out the side door, the music muted to a dull roar as the heavy oak falls shut behind us.

"Where did he...?" I'm glancing to the left when Cassie's hand goes slack in mine and she shouts.

"Darcy!"

He's running towards us, mouth open as he sprints all-out, pure terror on his face. I react instantly, my wings erupting from my back, a bright, dazzling red that matches my dress. I fly forward, ready to snatch Darcy away from whatever he's running from—when this giant thing leaps from out of nowhere landing between us.

It's man-shaped but I barely get a chance to glance at it before it hefts this huge ax in his hand and with one wild swing—

I scream and Cassie joins in. I whirl around, wrapping us both in my wings so we don't have to see.

But it's too late. That thing—a minotaur—separated Darcy's head from his body with one fatal swing.

And now, it's coming at us.

"I said, wait to strike!" A familiar voice—frustrated and angry—rings through the hall. I'd know it anywhere.

Ocypete has brought the monsters.

Almost instinctively, my wings retract at the sound of my flight instructor's voice. They know this person, trust her. With my wings away, I climb to my feet. Behind me, I hear Cassie whimpering.

Ocypete approaches me cautiously, a myriad of shadows behind her threading out into the light, one by one, each more hideous than the last. There's a minotaur, hairy and muscular, with horns that could impale me and a line of drool hanging from its mouth. A cyclops, his one eye rolling madly. A three-headed dog looms behind the cyclops, and beyond him a creature with a lion's head, wings, and goat feet. Behind him, just shadows, a silent, looming army ready to invade Mount Olympus Academy.

The dull thud of music from the dance floor continues; no one knows what just happened. I'm facing down this army alone.

"Why are you out here? All students should be inside!" Ocypete is in my face, so angry that I almost feel the need to explain myself. But then I catch of glimpse of the river of blood flowing out of Darcy's dead body.

"No," I say, smacking her finger out of my face. "What are *you* doing? You just killed a student!"

For the first time, I see something like uneasiness in Ocypete's face. "That wasn't me," she says slowly. "Not all of my people are as controlled—"

"You don't have control of your own army?" I shout at her, my voice breaking. "Darcy never hurt anybody," I say, my rage sliding quickly into tears. "He was kind..."

"I know, I know...listen, I know," Ocypete has one hand on my shoulder, my sobbing now mounting to match Cassie's, who is still behind me. Poor Cassie, who was right all along, and couldn't get anyone to listen.

"She knew," I say, wiping my nose. "Cassie knew this was going to happen."

"But she couldn't stop it, could she?" Pity asks. "That's war, kiddo. That's what I've been trying to teach you. It's ugly and it's terrible, and good, innocent people die because of it."

"People like Darcy?" I snap at her, shrugging out from under her comforting grip.

"Yes!" She insists. "Exactly! Didn't you listen to what I told you that day in my nest? The students are always the ones taking the brunt of the battles, serving as shields for the gods. That's why I've brought my monsters here, now. The gods are gathered. Let me—let us—end this."

I shake my head. "A monster killed my father! And you want me to believe you're the *good* guys?"

Ocypete shakes her head. "Edie, listen"—one claw clamps onto my wrist—"please, think. Vampires don't like shifters, right? You're on the same side, but there are issues, aren't there? Permanent, long-standing feuds?"

I remember the Wall of Weeping, and how a shifter killed a vampire there, kicking off the entire blood feud—a feud taking place on the same side of a much larger war.

I try to jerk my hand from Pity's claw, but she holds tight. "So?"

"So, it's the same for us. Levi and your father—"

But she doesn't get to finish. The music gets louder as someone opens the hall door, and then a scream blasts out. It's Tina, her fangs elongating at the sight of the monsters crowding the hall. She takes one glance at me, sees Pity's hand on my wrist, and lunges straight at me.

I'm stuck in place, facing down the vampire I knew would one day kill me, with an army of monsters behind me. It's the ultimate test and if I freeze—I'm dead.

My wings erupt, knocking Ocypete back as I turn, dashing for Cassie and scooping her from the floor. Tina is knocked sideways by one of my wings, tossed aside only moments before the monster army advances, and forces their way into the dance.

I come to a crashing halt at the end of the hall, Cassie limp and dazed in my arms, just in time to hear Ocypete's orders.

"Only the gods!" She shouts. "No harm to students!"

But as the screams fill my ears and the last monster stomps through the river of blood that used to run through Darcy, I know it's already too late.

32

I leave Cassie in the hall, and follow the screams.

The dance floor is chaos, shifter students already in their forms and vampires lunging for the throats of monsters. I fling open my wings, rising into the vaulted ceiling to look for Val. A hand grabs me, spins me, and I'm face to face with Greg, his bat wings out, but not fully shifted.

"Where's Val?" I shout at him.

"I don't know," he says. "We've got to get out of here."

"Out?" I yell, tearing my arm from his grip. "I'm not leaving everyone here to—"

"To what, Edie?" Greg yells. "What are you going to do? The other trackers already split. Our job is to find monsters, not fight them. Well look, I found them—they're everywhere!"

He points below, and I look just in time to see a centaur jam his thumbs into a werewolf's eye sockets, easily tearing his body in half with a casual jerk. Blood sprays and I shudder as the body shifts back into human form—a boy from one of my classes.

"No," I say. "I'm staying, to fight."

"Fight *how*?" Greg asks. "What are *you* going to do?"

"I don't know," I say, my voice shaky as Tina enters the room, unsteady on her feet after hitting her head against the wall in the hallway. I watch as she calmly assesses the chaos, straightens her dress, and dives in.

I wish I had her confidence. Wish I knew what I was, knew how to help.

My wings flutter around me, the part of myself that I am at ease with, the part I trust. I close my eyes, thinking of the other pair, the red ones deep inside me. It's time to stop locking them out. It's time to stop being afraid of what I am. The eyes are there, instantly, shifting and rolling, desperate to be released and join the fight. I don't look away. Instead, I focus, staring into myself.

They widen. Red. Pulsing. And suddenly I'm tearing, my skin separating and my fingers elongating, scales rippling up my arms as they flex, becoming more, becoming something *else*. I shriek in pain and Greg shifts completely, his bat-self making a quick exit as I writhe in mid-air, my spine exploding as a tail emerges, the scream that I began ending in something else.

A roar.

With it comes fire, and the feeling of bones popping through skin, sharpening to new edges, redefining into something new, something different. Spikes.

I lash my tail, a new balance achieved as I pull air into my lungs and exhale pure fire. I cry again, this time in exultation as I see my reflection in the windows.

Merilee was wrong. Cassie was wrong. Everyone was wrong.

I'm not a harpy, or a bat, and I sure as hell am no goddamn ostrich.

I am a dragon.

And I am very, very pissed.

I dive into the melee, first grabbing a siren in one clawed hand and pitching her out the window. Glass shatters as her black blood falls, and I circle, picking my next target. It's a cyclops, and he's got a cat-shifter in his grip, crushing her despite her frenzied clawing. I swoop, staggering the pair with my spiked tail. The girl rolls, as I knew she would—a cat always lands on its feet. But the cyclops is pure strength and brutality, with no grace. He stumbles and is off balance when I pass again, crunching him easily in my jaws, and throwing the remnants back down to the floor.

My human mind cowers at the violence and destruction, but my dragon-self embraces it. No, it enjoys the thrill of the kill. I roar a fiery explosion of satisfaction and power.

The cat gives me a nod, catches her breath, and goes back in.

It's pure chaos, blood—black and red—flowing everywhere. Hair is flying, fires have broken out. I come back to myself a bit and I search desperately for Val, but I can't see him anywhere.

I hear Ocypete shouting orders, still screaming not to harm students, but it's too late. It's a free-for-all with everyone fighting for their own lives. No one is pulling their punches.

I swivel, taking another pass of the room and searching for my next target when I see that the tables have all been turned—literally—and the gods are hiding beneath them. Themis is the only one not seeking cover. She's with Fern and another medic witch, grabbing injured students and pulling them aside. Confused, I don't make any kills on that pass, wondering why Kratos and Mr. Zee, Hermes and all of the other well-muscled gods aren't defending themselves.

Was Ocypete right? Are they really just using us?

I only have a second to consider it when I spot Val. He's backed into a corner and bleeding badly. A lion, crouched and ready to attack, facing him down. It's not a cat-shifter; I can tell by the way its coat moves—not naturally, but like it's made of actual gold, encased in metal and impervious to any weapon.

I may not know whose side I'm on, but I do know that anyone who hurts my fake ex-boyfriend is my enemy.

With that thought, I swoop.

And I rage.

"No!" There's a shriek as my path of my fire burns through monsters, sending a minotaur reeling. Suddenly, I feel the whisk of wings near mine, and Ocypete has landed in front of the lion, her arms outstretched.

"Edie! No!" She shouts. "Please! THINK!!"

But the lion springs at that moment, its muscular back legs releasing as it sails through the air, mouth wide, jaws snarling, claws splayed. Val's fangs are out and his arms are spread, waiting to meet it. I watch as the two of them roll, locked together.

I don't listen to Ocypete. I don't think. I act, spraying fire at the monster attacking Val—and the one standing in my way.

Ocypete ignites instantly, her old, brittle skin burning brightly as she ascends on fiery wings, hoping for escape. She doesn't reach the window, her burnt wings are feather-less before she's twenty feet in the air, and she falls, burning.

The lion is only scorched, but its back legs are alight and it runs in circles, frenzied. A hydra runs to it, spraying water to extinguish the fire, but with their leader gone, the fight is over. The lion sends one last snarl at me over his shoulder as he flees, harpies, gorgons, minotaurs and centaurs following in his wake. Some students chase after them, picking off a few in their retreat.

I sink, suddenly exhausted, my new body too heavy for my wings. I come down slowly, already transformed back into a human by the time I reach the floor, where Val finds me.

"You ruined another of my shirts," he says, and I see that his tuxedo t-shirt is charred to almost nothing.

"Sorry," I say. "I think I need to work more on my aim." I gulp. "And I think you're still smoldering."

He gives me one of his lopsided grins. "Nah, that's just a hot vampire thing."

A pathetic watery laugh comes out of me. "I wish everything would stop burning. It's all I can smell."

Even as I say it, a soft rain starts to fall, bringing with it the smell of green earth and fresh cut grass. I let the water flow down my face, wishing they were tears. But those seem to have burned away too.

Or maybe not.

"Edie," Val says.

Just that. Just my name as he takes a step closer, reaching for me.

One wobbly step is all it takes to get me close enough.

Then I collapse into his arms, and cry.

33

"Ms. Evans. Have a seat."

Mr. Zee's office looks like it belongs to another world. The walls are painted with murals of the sky and clouds. The furniture is stone with red pillows. Even his desk is weird, looking more like a sacrificial stone table than something that belongs in an office environment. He wears a toga and clutches a golden goblet.

I move forward and sit on the stone chair, glad for the comfy cushion.

Mr. Zee eyes me with interest. His gaze seems to see every inch of my skin and I feel suddenly naked. I shiver.

"So, you're the impossible girl? The dragon who saved the Academy."

"I did what I could," I mumbled. "I couldn't save everyone."

I can't help but think of Cassie, who is a total and complete wreck. After this meeting I'm going straight to her room so she doesn't have to be alone.

"No. The students' deaths are not your fault. Monsters

are merciless. You see now why the gods started this Academy."

I nod. "Pity—Ocypete—I thought she was my friend."

Mr. Zee shakes his head. "She fooled us all. I thought that although she was a monster, she had chosen the side of right. I will never make that mistake again." He takes a sip from his goblet. "Ocypete killed all those students. She set them on fire to make it look like you had done it. She wanted to make you an outcast so she could recruit you."

I am so stupid. Why didn't I report Pity when she told me she was a double agent? We could have avoided all this bloodshed. Darcy would still be alive.

Mr. Zee produces a file out of nowhere and looks through it. "It seems your father was a student here."

I fidget uncomfortably. What is in that file? Will Mr. Zee blame me for the circumstances of my birth?

"Hmmm, I don't remember your father. Or your mother. It seems they left to have children. How lucky for us that they did."

I blink. What does my file say? Not the truth, that's for sure. Did Themis change it to stay out of trouble?

"I'm sorry the monsters killed your father. Once an Academy student, always an Academy student. If they found him they would have wanted revenge."

He snaps the folder shut and it disappears. "A dragon! A creature of myth. How amazing. The Academy is so pleased to have you on our side. You will be our strongest weapon in this war."

I don't know what to say. I've gone from being the useless shifter who can't shift, to the hope of the gods.

"And I have some good news for you. We've found your mother. She's still in Greece."

I stand. Then sit. Then stand again. "You've found my mom?"

He nods. "It seems the monsters didn't kill her. They are probably using her for leverage. We can get a team together to extract her."

I collapse back into the chair, shakily. My mom is alive. It's more than I had hoped for. "And Mavis?" I ask, my voice wavering.

"Mavis?" Mr. Zee raises and eyebrow.

"My sister..."

He frowns. "There's no record of your sister. I'll have to dig a little deeper."

At least there's news of my mom. "When can I leave?" I ask.

"We'll have to put together a team. A tracker, a spy, a healer, and you. That's how these things work."

"I know who I want on my team," I tell him.

"You'll coordinate with Themis. She takes care of the details. I'm more of an ideas man." He waves his hand, indicating that he's dismissing me.

I leave his office and go directly to Themis'. She's not in, but I leave her a note that I have to talk with her immediately. I don't want to leave Cassie alone for too long, though, so I head back to the dorms.

In the courtyard students stare at me as I pass. I hear their whispers. That I'm a dragon. That I'm the most powerful shifter that ever was. That I saved the school.

It's bittersweet. I'm no longer seen as a loser, but at what cost? I catch a glimpse of Greg standing with his friends and detour. It must be hard for him too. He sees me coming and meets me half way.

I enfold him in a hug and when I look at his face there are tears in his eyes. "Greg, I'm so sorry. I couldn't..."

He shrugs. "It's not your fault." He gives me a playful punch on the shoulder. "So...you're a freaking dragon, huh? Badass."

I laugh. "Yeah, I guess you don't want to mate with me anymore, huh?"

His face reddens. "Oh no, I'm still into it. I mean, imagine a dragon-bat hybrid. Our kids would be awesome."

"My answer is still no," I say as kindly as possible.

"Well, can't blame a guy for trying." His eyes flick over my shoulder. "Great," he says rolling his eyes.

I turn to find Val. "Hey Greg, can I have a moment?"

"Yeah, sure, Edie." He reluctantly goes back to his friends.

"You look all healed up," I say to Val, feeling awkward after I'd cried all over him.

"Yeah," Val smiles crookedly and holds out his arms, displaying his perfect self, today wearing a t-shirt that reads *FLORIDA: THE BATH SALT STATE*. "Even better, after getting burned three times, the healers are sick of patching me up so they put a fireproof spell on me."

"Wow, so I guess that's one defense I won't be able to use against you."

"I wouldn't worry about that. I've got a feeling there are more tricks up your sleeve."

"Yeah," I agree, lamely.

And then we stand there, just sorta staring at each other.

"I should get back to Cassie," I say at last. "Was there something you wanted?"

I'm not sure what I'm hoping for. There's something between us, but—

"Val! *Come on* already!"

It's Tina. In her usual sneaky vampire way, she appeared out of nowhere.

"Tina." He shrugs her off where she has attached herself to his arm. "I was just saying good-bye to Edie."

"Good-bye?" I ask, suddenly feeling bereft. I look at Val, but it's Tina who answers.

"Spare me the drama. It's only a few weeks. Apparently, the gods sent notes to the clans last week. They're worried about the unusual uptick in interspecies dating and wanted our guardians to be aware of it."

"Are you in trouble?" Again, I ask Val. And again, Tina seems to think I'm talking to her.

"In trouble? Vampires don't get grounded." Tina rolls her eyes and somehow makes it look glamorous. "We're actually going home to celebrate. Val is being sworn to another vampire. It's like marriage, but way cooler, because—"

Knowing I'm a dragon makes me brave enough to cut Tina off. "Because you're vampires. Yeah, I get it." But my bravado doesn't last long, as Tina's words hit me and I realize what they mean. Somehow, as my throat grows tight with tears, I manage to squeak out, "Well congrats, Val. I'm... I really gotta get back to Cassie."

I spin and walk away as fast as I can without losing my last shreds of dignity. Anyway, after everything that happened the other night it seems dumb to care about something as small as a broken crush.

A hand grabs mine and whirls me around. I'm sure it's Val, finally ready to explain.

But instead it's Tina.

Again.

"He was never for you," she tells me in a low vicious voice.

I gulp and nod. "I know."

She nods too. And then suddenly relaxes her grip on my

hand. "By the way, I meant to say—you saved Val. I heard. I didn't see it. But whatever, it seems to be true, so... You're no longer the worst person on campus."

And with that—compliment?—she spins around to leave.

At least I'll get a break from her for a few weeks.

"Vee doesn't travel well, so you'll have to feed her for me," Tina calls back over her shoulder.

Before I can tell her 'no way, no how', she's already gone.

I take a detour through the dining hall on the way to Cassie's and am surprised by how easy it is to convince them to give me a giant tub of ice cream. There are apparently perks to being the hero of the day. If nothing else, Cassie and I can eat away our sorrows.

When I get to Cassie's room I'm surprised to find her mom, Merilee, there instead. Of course her mom would comfort her. Why would I think she'd be left alone? But where is Cassie? And why does Merilee look so stricken?

"What's going on?" I ask.

Merilee turns to me, a piece of paper clutched in her hands. "Edie, you have to help Cassie."

"Of course I will!" I say as she pushes the paper at me.

On it is a note, hastily scribbled but clearly in Cassie's handwriting.

The monsters want me. They're going to take me. Send help.

WANT MORE MOUNT OLYMPUS ACADEMY?

Pillage & Plague: Mount Olympus Academy Book 2
Available October 1st, 2019

Danger and mystery increase, as Edie attempts to survive a
long hot summer at Mount Olympus Academy.

PRE-ORDER NOW!!!!!

And there's even more...

Read a series of shorts set in the Mount Olympus Academy
world *before* Edie arrives on campus.

Sign up for MARLEY LYNN'S newsletter to get the first one:
RAGE & RUIN

and make sure you're receiving newsletters from

KATE KARYUS QUINN
and
DEMITRIA LUNETTA
so you receive all future stories as well!

ACKNOWLEDGMENTS

Thank you to Marin McGinnis for taking care of our copy edits!

Thank you to our cover designer Victoria @VC_BookCovers

And, of course, a big thank you to our families for putting up with us crazy writers.

ABOUT THE AUTHORS

DEMITRIA LUNETTA is the author of the YA books THE FADE, BAD BLOOD, and the sci-fi duology, IN THE AFTER and IN THE END. She is also an editor and contributing author for the YA anthology, AMONG THE SHADOWS: 13 STORIES OF DARKNESS & LIGHT. Find her at www.demitrialunetta.com for news on upcoming projects and releases.

KATE KARYUS QUINN is an avid reader and menthol chapstick addict with a BFA in theater and an MFA in film and television production. She lives in Buffalo, New York with her husband, three children, and one enormous dog. She has three young adult novels published with HarperTeen: ANOTHER LITTLE PIECE, (DON'T YOU) FORGET ABOUT ME, AND DOWN WITH THE SHINE. She also recently released her first adult novel, THE SHOW MUST GO ON, a romantic comedy. Find out more at www.katekaryusquinn.com

MARLEY LYNN is a lost child of the gods, who waits on the shores of Lake Erie for her parents to bring her home. In the meantime, she contents herself with reading, writing, and gardening. Find out more at www.MarleyLynn.com

ALSO BY THE AUTHORS

IN THE AFTER by Demitria Lunetta

In debut author Demitria Lunetta's heart-pounding thriller, one girl must fight for her survival in a world overrun by violent, deadly creatures. Perfect for fans of *The 5th Wave* and *A Quiet Place*.

Amy Harris's life changed forever when They took over. Her parents—vanished. The government—obsolete. Societal structure —nonexistent. No one knows where They came from, but these vicious creatures have been rapidly devouring mankind since They appeared.

With fierce survivor instincts, Amy manages to stay alive—and even rescues "Baby," a toddler who was left behind. After years of hiding, they are miraculously rescued and taken to New Hope. On the surface, it appears to be a safe haven for survivors. But there are dark and twisted secrets lurking beneath that could have Amy and Baby paying with not only their freedom . . . but also their lives.

BUY NOW

DOWN WITH THE SHINE by Kate Karyus Quinn

Think twice before you make a wish in this imaginative, twisted, and witty new novel from the author of *Another Little Piece*.

When Lennie brings a few jars of her uncles' moonshine to Michaela Gordon's house party, she has everyone who drinks it make a wish. It's tradition. So is the toast her uncles taught her: "May all your wishes come true, or at least just this one."

The thing is, those words aren't just a tradition. The next morning, every wish—no matter how crazy—comes true. And most of them turn out bad. But once granted, a wish can't be unmade . . .

BUY NOW

AMONG THE SHADOWS: Thirteen Stories of Darkness & Light

Edited and with stories written by Demitria Lunetta and Kate Karyus Quinn

Even the lightest hearts have shaded corners to hide the black thoughts that come at night. Experience the darker side of YA as 13 authors explore the places that others prefer to leave among the shadows.

BUY NOW

BETTY BITES BACK

FEMINIST FICTION TO FRIGHTEN THE PATRIARCHY!

Edited and with stories written by Demitria Lunetta and Kate Karyus Quinn

Behind every successful man is a strong woman... but in these stories, she might be about to plant a knife in his spine. The characters in this anthology are fed up - tired of being held back, held down, held accountable - by the misogyny of the system. They're ready to resist by biting back in their own individual ways, be it through magic, murder, technology, teeth, pitfalls and even... potlucks. Join sixteen writers as they explore feminism in fantasy, science-fiction, fractured fairy-tales, historical settings, and the all-too-familiar chauvinist contemporary world.

BUY NOW

11970624R00134

Made in the USA
Monee, IL
19 September 2019